Superstars of the Galaxy:
An Explosive Entrance

Written by William Craig Eason II
Edited by Leah Lakins

The contents of this work, including, but not limited to, the accuracy of events, people, and places depicted; opinions expressed; permission to use previously published materials included; and any advice given or actions advocated are solely the responsibility of the author, who assumes all liability for said work and indemnifies the publisher against any claims stemming from publication of the work.

Based on characters created by William Craig Eason II, and Amy L. Eason.

Dorrance Publishing Co
585 Alpha Drive
Pittsburgh, PA 15238
Visit our website at *www.dorrancebookstore.com*

ISBN: 978-1-4809-3389-7
eISBN: 978-1-4809-3366-8

Chapter 1

As the flames of the burning city buildings began to fade, Lyonne, the capital of the Planet York III, took on an ominous look as a foreboding, black sky moved over the city. The crying and screaming of the native inhabitants subsided for now.

Two patrol guards leaned against the smooth stonewall of one of the watch-towers at the corner of the city wall. Captain Nammill, the senior guard in the duo, chuckled to himself as he witnessed an old woman on her knees in the middle of one of the main city streets, sobbing uncontrollably over a dead man's body. Nam-mill's tall frame allowed him to see over the wall's fortification barriers and into the city. The officers' insignias and medals reflected what little light was left from the city's flames.

"Sooner or later they're going to learn," Nammill said, smirking.

"Yes, sir, Captain Nammill," said Officer John Vaggs, the younger and more cautious guard who was choosing his words very carefully.

"I don't know why they don't just leave this forsaken place," he sneered. "They are stupid to stay and subject themselves to this. The old regime will never return."

"This is their home, sir."

Nammill shrugged off John's naivete. "At least you were smart enough to join the winning side before they killed you, too. It's funny what someone will do to save his own life."

John smartly decided to keep his commentary to himself and remained quiet. He knew that many of the natives had died defending their home city, their home world, and their way of life. He continually felt guilty for what he had done, but he wasn't the only one who saw the inevitable ending to the war.

John snapped out of his reverie when he heard Nammill yell, "Vaggs, did you do your scan from the last hour?" He could tell the captain's tone was serious and formal.

"Yes, sir."

"Well, why don't you do another? I'm going to take a short break."

John sensed some deception in the captain's voice. He guessed that Nammill was craving yet another smoke. However, the act of leaving any military post was prohibited while on patrol duty. The two still had five hours before their next break, but he knew Nammill was not going to wait that long.

Nammill turned toward him again. "Go on, now. You never know what might be worth reporting out there." He shooed John with his head.

John quickly slipped passed the captain and into the nearest watchtower. He could faintly hear the captain flicking a cigar lighter as he ascended the rickety, wooden ladder to the top of the bastion. The bastion wall was about forty feet high, but John was a very athletic soldier, and he climbed the ladder with minimal effort. He climbed onto the flat base of the bastion and kicked the hatch closed behind him. When he reached the top, he grabbed his night scanners from the left side of his uniform and raised them to his eyes.

"Gah!" John said aloud.

He jerked the scanners from his eyes clumsily. He blinked wildly to clear the sunspots gathering in his eyes from what he saw.

"I must have set the wrong time," he muttered to himself, shaking his head at his own stupidity.

He glanced at the underside of the scanners, and he stared at the glowing control panel and the digital readout. The setting was correct, but this was a strange readout for this time of day. John raised the scanners to his eyes again.

"Geez!" he said, squinting his eyes from the blinding light. "What's going on?"

John looked up in the direction of the blinding light without the scanners. He was shocked at the sight that lay before his eyes. There was a tiny, flickering light, gleaming like a distant star on the horizon. This was the first sign of life's existence in the vast darkness that was nightfall on Planet York III in quite some time. He wondered how no one else had seen it.

John descended the ladder with the intention of informing his immediate superior. But as he reached the city wall floor, he hesitated. This light, even though it had no action associated with it, was the first sign of any native rebelliousness in many years. One of the new regime's laws prohibited unauthorized activity after nightfall. This law was created originally to protect the military from nightly ambushes of any foreign or alien species. While his conscience was beginning to feel revived, John was dreading the deadly dilemma that now lay before him. If he did not inform Nammill of the sighting, he could be caught in a lie if the patrol officer during the next shift noticed the light. He could put himself in further danger by waiting too long to report his finding and thus be seen as an accomplice for these illegal activities.

There was no acceptable way out of this predicament, yet he had to make a decision quickly. The longer he waited, the more dangerous the situation would become for everyone.

Dr. Sylvester Nolan startled himself and coughed violently. He had fallen asleep and wasn't sure how long he had been out.

"Damn," he said.

Dr. Nolan had not been up this late in years. Apparently his scientific journals were not very interesting, ironically not even to himself. He looked at the page number of the old journal.

"Five, only page five," he muttered.

He glanced at the clock mounted on the kitchen wall.

"Just a short nap for the old noggin," he chuckled lightly to himself.

He glanced at the picture of his long-lost wife hanging loosely on the wall next to the front door. It was a picture of a smiling middle-aged woman with short, curly, light brown hair and modest makeup on her face.

"I think I can do it tonight, Neptune," Dr. Nolan said, hoping she could hear his voice wherever she was.

Dr. Nolan, a once prominent professor of biology at Planet York III's most prestigious university, stood up slowly from his rocking chair. The notebook he was reading before he dozed off fell from his knees. The sound scared a few Udderlicks, the large beetle-like insects with long tentacles and legs that were underneath his rocking chair. The pests ran and hid in a dark corner of the living room. They made a chattering sound as they contemplated their next move. They were attracted to the candles in his kitchen.

"Nasty things," he murmured with disgust.

He headed toward the kitchen and stopped in front of a tiny table. He stared at the homemade contraption that was the centerpiece of his table. The contraption was a rectangular glass tank, about a foot deep by two feet wide and a foot long, that held ten air-sealed bio-tubes. The tubes contained dangerous organisms that floated in lukewarm water. A net floated just underneath the tubes and its corners were attached to two three-inch long explosive devices perched at the edge of the table.

Dr. Nolan smiled at his invention. "I'm not crazy yet," he said with a laugh reminiscent of a mad scientist.

He turned and looked at Neptune's picture again.

"What should we name each one?"

He turned back to the floating bio-tubes. The organism in the third tube leaped to the top and fell back to the bottom, causing ripples in the tank water.

"Ooh, that's a feisty one," he said. "Let's call her Hynyia. The comet Hynyia will be passing over soon." He paused. "But what if it's a boy?"

Suddenly there was a knock at his front door, and Dr. Nolan's heart jumped. He couldn't let anyone see his experiment. While no one except for his long-time friend and co-worker, Professor Benni, would actually know what the intended purpose of the contraption was, there was a great risk that he would be reported to the capital city police for violating his license. Planet York III had strict laws regulating people like Dr. Nolan, who performed experiments that could possibly harm people. While the professor had never had an experiment go wrong in his thirty years of practice, the new regime didn't seem to think that that was reason enough to let him continue his work.

There was another knock at the door, this time a little louder. The doctor wasn't expecting any visitors this late in the evening, and he had no living family anywhere nearby. Dr. Nolan searched frantically around the room for something to cover the tank.

"Just a minute," he said, trying to sound as if he'd been awoken from his sleep.

Then he heard the lock begin to jiggle. Someone was breaking into his house, and he had no way to hide this huge contraption. As he turned to go into his bedroom to grab the sheet off of his cot, he could see the lock on the front door slide to the unlocked position. Dr. Nolan couldn't bear for his night to end this way.

John cautiously approached Nammill, who was suspiciously positioned next to the wall of the nearest bastion. As he drew nearer, he could see the captain putting out his cigar on the city wall railing. Nammill turned toward John with a grunt and slight cough.

"What do you want?" he said angrily. "That scan couldn't have been more than ten minutes."

"Um, sir," John said quietly.

"Well?"

"There appears to be an infraction of night code seven-three-eight about thirty miles northwest."

Nammill turned to look in the direction of the infraction. In the distance he could see a tiny light flickering just above the horizon line. He stared harder, scowling his brows. He was more shocked than surprised that John had anything to report during his scan. It had been many moons since something unusual had happened on Planet York III after the new regime had taken over.

"What is that?" he asked.

Nammill whipped his night scanner up to his eyes, leaned forward over the wall's three-foot-high stone railing, and adjusted the scanner's settings. There were a few tense moments of silence between the two guards as Nammill took a closer look into the scanner. He turned toward John.

"What time did the infraction incur?"

Nammill put his right wrist to his mouth preparing to communicate their findings to the main military watch office.

John knew this question was a trap. Admitting that he didn't know when the incident occurred meant he wasn't doing his job and this could possibly mean being relieved of his military rank and position. This would also mean that he was concealing information from the regime, which could make him a suspected accomplice. Reporting the time incorrectly would also put Nammill under the microscope, and the worse thing John could ever do is make Nammill responsible for his mistake.

Nammill glared at John, demanding an answer. John looked down at his timekeeper on his right wrist.

"Zero-zero-seventy-five minutes after sunset," he finally said.

Nammill's communicator beeped. "This is Captain Nammill reporting to base."

There was a short hiss and then a mechanical voice said, "Go ahead, unit five-three-alpha."

"I have an infraction of night code seven-three-eight located about thirty miles northwest. It appears to be near the town of Ombrick."

"Processing," the mechanical voice replied.

"Time of infraction?" questioned the voice a moment later.

"Zero-zero-seventy-five minutes after sunset," Nammill repeated. "Course of action needed?"

"One moment," the voice said, apparently in no hurry.

The two guards stood there, slightly nervous about their own fates even more so than whatever had caused the infraction.

"Take action immediately," the voice commanded. "Question and arrest any suspects at location now. Ensure that there are no threats to the regime and remove the illumination. No other options available."

Just before Nammill turned off the communicator, the mechanical voice crackled through the receiver and said, "And don't mess up this time, Captain."

Nammill glared at John with a disgusted look. He was angry about the situation in which they had found themselves. He fastened his night scanner to his belt and motioned for John to follow him over to the lift that would lower them to the ground level of the bastion. John followed reluctantly.

Once the lift slammed onto the stone floor underneath the bastion, Nammill turned on his communicator. "Base, this is Captain Nammill requesting backup for investigation procedure."

Both guards began to walk toward the nearest depot in search of a transport. Nammill didn't get his hopes up too high for his backup request to be fulfilled. This military regime wasn't too forgiving of insolent officers and the groups that they controlled. He wouldn't be surprised if the base simply sent him and John out into the night to die at the hands of rioting civilians. The other military commanders would consider that an appropriate payment for this mistake.

Nammill's communicator crackled, "Backup is already waiting. Report to depot three-bravo-six."

John's eyes perked up when he overheard the response. He wasn't sure what that statement really implied. Either the backup was being sent because the two guards were no longer trusted, or the backup was really an executioner preparing to kill them after everything checked out normally at the infraction location. John was going to ask Nammill what to do, but it was obvious that he didn't want to be bothered now by petty questions about their own survival. He decided to remain quiet.

Both guards walked briskly through a sparsely lit alley that paralleled the city wall. As they neared their assigned depot, they could see the outline of a large figure leaning against the depot entrance. The figure appeared to be humanoid in size and stature, but definitely not human in species.

Once Nammill reached the depot door, a sheath of light revealed that the creature was an eight-foot tall, approximately four hundred-pound alien with a triangular head. The alien had purple, oval-shaped eyes, sharp, bright white teeth that hung from the sides of its mouth, and nostrils that protruded almost a foot away from its head. The male creature wore armor around his chest, a tool belt around his waist with several compartments, large, thick leather boots on his feet, and a large weapon attached to his back.

Nammill ignored the creature as he typed in the depot entry code onto the panel on the left side of the door. Under any normal circumstances, the two guards would have questioned the being, but this was no normal circumstance. They both secretly hoped this alien was the backup, not part of the problem. Both he and John could hear the alien's deep, erratic breathing, but the being made no motion to communicate with either of them. It just stood there as if waiting for something to happen.

The captain mistyped the code to the depot door and mumbled to himself. The panel flashed red a few times then turned yellow. The alien grunted toward the officers.

John unwillingly looked at the ominous ugly figure. This massive creature intimidated him, but he had to stay clear and focused during this awkward situation. It was making him nervous.

"Did you say something?" John asked the alien.

The captain mistyped the code to the door again.

"Blast it," Nammill exclaimed nervously.

The alien lifted his black scaly hand to adjust something under its chin. There was a static sound like a radio adjusting then a low, clear humming noise.

"Sorry about that," the alien said with a fabricated, deep male voice. "I forgot to tune my translation channel."

Both the guards felt a little relief that at least the alien was not being hostile for now.

"The code's been changed," he said.

Nammill immediately became concerned. He didn't have time to worry about the reasons for the action, and why he wasn't notified about the change. The alien moved slowly in front of the captain and pulled a key device from his belt pouch. He inserted the key into a slot; the panel lights flickered yellow, and then turned a solid green. The depot door slid open.

"After you," the alien said.

John walked briskly passed the alien, whom he now deduced was a mercenary hired for special small operations. He walked outside of the depot and looked for their transport. Nammill came out next, followed closely by the alien. John scouted the first few transports he saw. He hoped that this mission wouldn't produce any dangerous situations, and he selected the first small transport he found. John jumped into the driver seat and pushed the initiation button. He placed his key into the unlock slot underneath the steering wheel and checked the energy gauge.

"This one's ready to go," John yelled over his shoulder.

"Works for me," the alien said.

Nammill remained silent, pondering the procedure they should follow once they reached their destination. This was assuming that they would actually reach their destination.

The alien barely beat the captain to the vehicle and he hoisted himself into the back seat. The entire transport was lowered from the weight of the alien. Nammill glared at John as he jumped into the co-pilot seat. He was obviously angry as he turned on the navigation scope and the front lights. John pushed the button to open the launch doors to the depot and started the engine.

"Ready your weapons, boys," the alien said.

"It will take us thirty minutes to get to Ombrick," Nammill replied. "There's no hurry."

"You never know what's going to happen along the journey," the alien responded with a menacing tone.

Nammill turned to John and motioned for him to begin the drive to their destination. The captain turned back to look at the navigation panel. As the engines kicked into high gear and the transport began to hover over the solid metal floor of the depot, Nammill used the engine's noise to disguise the clicking sound as he loosened his nucleon pistol from his belt buckle. He placed the weapon cautiously in his lap, his finger on the trigger.

Chapter 2

As Dr. Nolan hobbled back into the kitchen, he flung the bed sheet over the kitchen table just as the front door opened. A gust of wind blew through the house, causing the sheet to settle on one side of the tank. Dr. Nolan kept his back facing the front door, hoping that the intruder wasn't going to kill him.

"Professor?" said a soft, female voice from behind the door.

The front door shut quietly and the lock was fastened. Dr. Nolan recognized that it was the voice of his long-time assistant, Vara Cottsak. He breathed a sigh of relief. He adjusted the bed sheet on the left of the glass tank to completely cover it.

Vara stepped closer to the professor, cautiously sensing his agitation. "Are you alright?"

Dr. Nolan cleared his throat. In his best calm voice, he turned around and said, "Yes, why do you ask?"

"You're breathing very heavily," she said, trying to peek around the professor at the thing hidden on the kitchen table.

"You startled me. That's all, Vara." He was surprised that she was in his home. Her shift ended hours ago.

As Vara shifted to get around the professor to get a closer look at the mysterious thing on the table, Dr. Nolan shifted along with her. The scene was awkward, neither knowing what to say or do. But both of them obviously had their attention centered around the hidden contraption on the table, each for different reasons.

"Why are you here, Vara?"

"I was worried about you," she said, turning her gaze to the old man's weathered face.

"Why are you worried? I'm a grown man who can take care of himself."

"Because it's passed curfew."

Dr. Nolan felt a hollow pit form in his stomach. He glanced over his shoulder at the clock on his wall. It was almost two hours after curfew, and on Planet York III, curfew meant that everyone should be at home with the lights out. The realization of his mistake was painfully obvious now. He couldn't move. He just stared at the clock.

"Dr. Nolan?"

Dr. Nolan snapped out of his short trance, and he now knew what he had to do.

"Vara," he said in a commanding tone. "I need your help."

"I thought so," she replied in a motherly tone, even though she was much younger than the professor.

"Can you go outside and see if there are any patrol vehicles headed this way?" Dr. Nolan was hoping for the best, but he feared the worst.

Vara ran to the front door, unlocked the latch, and stepped outside. Dr. Nolan quickly ripped the sheet off of the glass tank and began to ponder the quickest way to disassemble it. As he was scouring the contraption, Vara flew back in to the house. She shut the front door behind her loudly and flipped the lock. Her eyes were filled with fear.

"What?" Dr. Nolan demanded.

"Two transport lights, not more than five miles from here," Vara said petrified.

Dr. Nolan could sense that Vara feared for her own safety as well as his. He couldn't think fast enough. His brain was clouded with thoughts of his wife and the experiment stationed in the middle of his house. He couldn't stop thinking about how sad it was to have his only love die so soon and not have any living thing left behind to ease the pain. All of his hard work was about to be taken away by guards who didn't care anything about him or this planet he once called home.

"Professor!" Vara screamed.

"Quick!" Dr. Nolan said. "Into the bedroom and shut the door."

Vara quickly slid into the dark bedroom, leaving the door behind her slightly ajar. Dr. Nolan felt a glimmer of hope.

"At least one of us might get out of this alive," he muttered to himself.

He then turned his attention to the contraption. The glow from the tank was radiating through the house's main rooms. He had to find a way to tone everything down. It was too obvious.

"I should just put the darn thing on the floor," he said to himself.

Dr. Nolan wrapped his wrinkly, old arms around the sheet that covered the glass tank and lifted it. He struggled and moaned under its weight. Vara ran out of the bedroom to help him.

"Vara! What are you doing?" he bellowed.

"Helping," she said as she grabbed the other side of the sheet to keep the doctor from falling over.

The two of them cautiously lowered the tank onto the wooden floor. They slid the contraption underneath the table, causing some hidden Udderlicks to scatter. Vara shivered at the pests, but remained silent.

Suddenly there was a hard pounding at the door.

"This is Patrol Night Scan. Open the door," said an angry male voice.

"Hurry," the professor whispered to Vara pointing to the bedroom.

They both stood up abruptly, bumping the table and knocking some candles onto the floor. Dr. Nolan blew out a few candles in the room to make the scene look less radiant. Just as Vara slipped back into the bedroom, another knock sounded at the door.

"This is your last warning! Open up or we will force entry!"

"Just a moment," Dr. Nolan said, faking a sleepy voice.

Outside the door, John was shaking from nervousness, his weapon aimed at the door and ready to fire. Nammill motioned with his hand for the alien mercenary to stand to the right of the front door. This strategic move was just in case the insurgents inside decided to bolt through the front door upon entry.

As the captain lifted his right foot to force the old wooden door open, it cracked a bit and an old, shriveled face peeked out.

"Yes, officer?" Dr. Nolan asked, trying to sound amazed at their presence.

Nammill pushed the front door open, knocking the doctor to the floor. Dr. Nolan landed hard, causing a sharp pain in his hip. Closely followed by the alien mercenary, Nammill quickly scanned the small, dusty living room. John, with a regretful look on his face, helped the old man to his feet.

"That was uncalled for," Dr. Nolan said, while rubbing his bruised hip. "What do you want?"

"I'm asking the questions here tonight," Nammill replied as he grabbed his datapad from his right front pocket. He pressed a few buttons and asked, "Dr. Nolan, is it?"

Dr. Nolan said nothing.

Vara, who was peeking through a small crack in the bedroom door, was trying to think of a way to get out of this mess. As soon as she saw the alien mercenary, she was careful not to make any extra noises or movements. These kinds of aliens were known for having excellent hunting and tracking skills. A mere sniffle from her would alert this being to her presence in seconds.

The alien mercenary began to scan the rooms looking for anything suspicious or illegal. It lifted its nostrils in an attempt to pick up any unique odors. It headed toward a corner wall just between the kitchen and the bedroom.

"What exactly are you doing in here, doctor?" Nammill asked. "You are aware that you are in violation of code seven-three-eight?"

"What?" Dr. Nolan asked, playing dumb.

"Curfew," the captain said with an exasperated tone. He strolled toward Dr. Nolan and leaned in close enough to smell his breath. "Don't play innocent with me."

"Sir," John yelled.

Nammill was annoyed by the interruption, but he didn't divert his gaze from Dr. Nolan's suspicious eyes. "What, Vaggs?"

The officer motioned his head toward the alien mercenary who was standing in front of the bedroom door, not moving at all. Its scaly hand was raised as if it was trying to hear some soft noise from within the dark room. Nammill turned and walked quickly but quietly to the alien mercenary. He stood a few feet behind the massive creature.

"What is it?" he asked.

There was a short pause.

"Fire!" he screamed as he whirled around.

The cloth that covered the tank was ablaze. The flames were spreading rapidly to the old wooden kitchen counters and cabinets. The alien bolted passed Nammill, knocking him to the floor, and shoved John and Dr. Nolan aside as he ran out the front door.

Vara could begin to smell the smoke on the other side of the door. The light from the fire began to shine through the cracks. She turned around, looking for a way out of the room. The window over the bed was small, but she thought that she could fit. She ran over to open it, but it was jammed. She tugged hard, struggling for her survival.

The flames began to race through the kitchen and into the living room. Nammill stood up, coughing from the smoke. He motioned for John to get out of the house. John nodded and ran out, leaving Dr. Nolan, who fell to the floor.

"Stupid!" Nammill screamed at John, angry at the misunderstanding.

Dr. Nolan was on the floor, frozen, as he watched his whole life disintegrate in a fire. Tears streamed down his face as pictures of his beloved Neptune were engulfed in the flames. His heart pounded as holes began to form in the roof of his house, revealing the star-filled, night sky. He grew angry as years of his hard work began to collapse at his feet. He turned toward the captain, who was standing near the bedroom coughing.

As the captain reached in his back pocket for his stun collar, the old doctor charged at him, knocking him into the kitchen.

"You have no idea what you've done!" Dr. Nolan screamed as he began slapping Nammill on the face, like a petulant child.

Nammill turned his head and repeatedly blocked the blows from Dr. Nolan. The captain rotated his body to grab the stun collar. Dr. Nolan, seemingly unaffected by the heat and smoke, noticed the captain's attempt to subdue him and he grabbed the collar out of his hands.

"You'd better not!" Nammill shouted, sensing the old man's next move.

Dr. Nolan snapped the collar on the captain's leg right above the ankle, rendering most of his lower body muscles useless. The doctor stood up over Nammill. Captain Nammill was afraid Dr. Nolan would leave him there to die.

Dr. Nolan glanced into his kitchen, where he could barely see the tank. The table wouldn't hide the contraption for much longer. When the fire reached it, a huge explosion would certainly occur. He turned to leave the captain for dead. As he exited his house, he saw the only remaining picture of Neptune near the front door. Dr. Nolan grabbed the picture off of the wall and tucked it underneath his arm. He thought about his wife's zest for life and inherent happiness. He realized he couldn't leave the captain there to die.

Amidst coughs and pants, Dr. Nolan dragged the conscious but immobile captain out of the house into the barren city street. He turned to look at his home as it disappeared into his past. He cringed as he heard the glass tank crack and break on the floor in the blaze. He waited a few moments, then the rockets began to launch. There was a series of tiny explosions, too many to see them all at once. Dr. Nolan was pained as his experiment failed before his aged eyes. He could hear sirens in the distance, surely coming to extinguish the fire his intruders had caused. He realized he had made a mistake.

"Vara!" he gasped.

Just as he started to reenter the fiery mess, someone hit the back of his head with a heavy object. Dr. Nolan fell to the ground, barely conscious, watching the flames.

Vara could not breathe, only cough. The smoke was consuming the little bedroom at a deathly pace. She kept tugging at the window, but nothing happened. She had to think of some other way out. She turned toward the bedroom door. It was now ablaze, blocking her only other way out. She slipped and fell next to the old man's bed. She could hear faint sirens in the distance. Vara, feeling the life leaving her, could not think clearly. She pulled a torn and dirty sheet off of the bed, covered most of her upper body and face, and rolled underneath the furniture. She closed her eyes, mostly because of fear and anticipation of death, but also because the smoke was making them itch very badly. With her head covered, Vara heard the house crumbling all around her. Amidst the crackling fire she could hear something that sounded like fireworks. She would surely burn to death in Dr. Nolan's house.

Vara screamed as a huge piece of the bedroom wall fell next to the bed. She curled up in a tight ball. Sparks from the wall lit the bed and sheets on fire. Vara frantically smacked at the tiny flames. She peeked out from the sheet, but could only see bright orange and white flames of fire. The heat from the fire was starting to cook Vara's skin.

Suddenly something pulled Vara out from underneath the bed. She hit her head on the underside of the bed as this unknown force dragged her out of the house and into the city street.

"Sorry about that, madam," said an apologetic male voice from above.

Vara realized she couldn't see through the bed sheet. She cautiously removed it. The man who had just spoken to her ran back into the burning house. Another man knelt beside her.

"Madam? Are you ok?" the other man asked.

Vara could see the fire rescue emblem on his left shoulder. He lifted a lukewarm towel up to her nose and pinched it tightly.

"I think you bumped your nose on the way out," he said. "It could have been worse."

A few more rescue squad members rushed past Vara. The fire was beginning to calm down. Vara suddenly felt dizzy. She moaned from the tiredness and the pain from the bump on her head. She leaned her head into the rescue worker's chest.

"I guess Officer Ferrell was too rough getting you out of there," he said.

He laid her down gently on a folded up towel in the stone street. He untied his rescue kit and pulled out some gauze and tape. He parted her hair and placed some warm, damp gauze on Vara's bump.

As she lay there, Vara looked up into the dark sky, her eyes still burning from the smoke. She could see tiny, white and blue explosions in the distance. She counted a few, hoping that she could tell the professor about his brilliant display later.

"Those are beautiful fireworks."

The squad member looked up to see what Vara was talking about.

"Those are some impressive explosions," he agreed.

"How far do you think they went?" Vara asked.

"I suppose a few of the powerful ones left this atmosphere. Like that one," he said, pointing to a very tiny explosion. It was so small that it looked like a star exploding millions of miles away. Hundreds of small objects that looked like falling stars were the only aftermath of the display.

The mile-long spaceship cast an ominous shadow as it cruised past the seventh moon of Killak. Many people feared these gigantic vessels, not only because of the sheer size, but its firepower was unmatched by any ship within thousands of sectors. The Ray Patroller, which belonged to the organization known as Sci-Fi Force, had been in this current sector for the past three hundred and fifty years. Its crewmembers had come and gone, much like the ebb and flow of any large organization. The people aboard now had been fortunate to see many recent years of peace and rest. However, things were about to change.

Captain Beri Onex was performing a routine scan on her gamma screen. It allowed the crewmembers to see any type of battle action light thousands of leagues away. The gamma screen also measured sudden temperature changes in deep space across multiple galaxies. The original use was to monitor the death of stars. Civilizations that depended on certain stars for energy could leave their native planets years before their home was uninhabitable. Beri was finishing her routine viewing into the gamma scope when she noticed something different toward the top right of her screen.

"Strange," she muttered to herself.

Her superior, Chief Captain Sheep, heard her observation from the far side of the room. "Is there something to report, Captain?"

"Come take a look at this, sir,"

Chief Captain Sheep walked briskly across the sleek, red, metal floor and leaned over Beri's left shoulder to get a closer look at the screen.

"Very interesting," he said staring at the thousands of tiny lights flickering on her screen. "There's no way that those can all be stars."

"What else could it be?"

"Can you run a length shot on it? Those flashes appear very far away. They might be in someone else's jurisdiction."

"I'll try," she said. "It's going to be difficult. They are moving quickly."

Beri was not known for her gunnery skills, but she would have to work with what she had. She took hold of the shifter underneath her desk and a little red circle showed up on her green screen. She placed her thumb on top of the shifter and prepared to take a shot. She moved the circle over one of the flashing lights. The screen lit up with a bright blue circle and she took the first shot she had. She held her breath.

"Good shot, Captain."

Now the entire room was interested in what was happening near Beri's seat. They were all holding their breath when a beep sounded near Officer Ty Chu's seat.

"I got something," Ty said, sounding excited, anticipating a little action. He spun around in his chair and stared at his computer monitor. "It's in the QX sector," he confirmed with some confidence. He whirled to another terminal and typed something very quickly on the keyboard. "That's Admiral Raynger's sector."

"If they were fighting someone, they would have already sent us a distress or backup signal," Sheep mused aloud. "Officer Chu, get the Lieutenant Commander on the line."

Ty picked up his headset and commanded, "Main Bridge, Chief Captain Sheep has a report for current patrol shift."

The room's main speaker's crackled. "Proceed, Chief Captain," a booming voice said.

Sheep took Ty's headset and said, "Lieutenant Commander, we have picked up some unusual action in the QX sector. It appears to be battle activity but we are not sure. When was the last time we received a signal from them?"

There was a pause and then the sound of some typing.

"We last received contact from Admiral Raynger ten hours ago. He gave us his usual report," the voice said, seeming unconcerned.

"Do you mind if we try to contact him again?"

"Not a problem, Chief Captain. Just a moment."

The loud speakers in the room crackled as the signal was changed to include the Admiral from the QX sector.

"This is Ray Patroller nine-nine-gamma-five inquiring about spatial activity near the QX sector. Anything to report, Admiral?"

There was a long pause. Chief Captain Sheep began to get nervous.

"Nothing to report," the robotic voice said over the signal.

The Captain was puzzled. "Lieutenant Commander, can we at least ask if they saw what we saw?"

"Proceed," the voice affirmed.

"Admiral, we detected unusual flashes of light in or near your jurisdiction. Was this some type of exercise or weapons test?" Sheep asked, hoping he did not sound stupid in front of his subordinates.

There was another long pause.

"Nothing to report," the voice said again.

Beri, along with most of the people in the room, noticed something very strange and suspicious about the responses. She risked stepping out of rank as she stood up in her chair and asked the Admiral, "Sir, when was your last report?"

"Captain!" Sheep scolded. "That was out of line!"

"Nothing to report," the voice said again through the speakers.

Beri sat down in her seat with a smirk on her face. She turned back to her monitor. The tiny lights were still flickering but appearing to fade.

"Chief Captain Sheep," commanded the booming voice. "This requires an investigation!"

Beri loaded the last survival pack into the Light Ripper. This spaceship was sleek and fast, perfect for small rescue, reconnaissance, and routine missions. It had one small gun and three boost thrusters for quick maneuvering. It could only carry six total people, and for this mission there would be six Sci-Fi agents aboard.

Beri had volunteered for the mission, and Chief Captain Sheep chose to have her lead it as well. She had been assigned five agents: Officer Ty Chu, Senior Agent Penn Jovic, and Junior Agents Lilac Wenn, Vince Filtreth, and Hilton Rrorr. She scanned her crew.

"You couldn't get a more junior group if it was the lottery from hell," Ty said under his breath to Beri. He was disgusted by the people Chief Captain Sheep selected to join them on this mission.

"If we are such a junior team, then what does that say about you?" Vince said as he climbed into the ship.

"They obviously don't think there is any danger," Beri said quietly in response.

The lower ranking Sci-Fi agents were often very brutally honest with each other, sometimes too honest. Ty didn't have much respect for Beri, and he didn't hesitate to let the others see his displeasure with her leadership.

"Junior Agent Rrorr, how do the thrusters look?" Beri asked as she climbed into the cockpit.

Hilton poked his dusty head around from the back of the ship. "The right and middle thrusters are great, but the left one needs some work. I can fix it when we get to the QX sector. It shouldn't delay the trip."

"Hopefully the gun works," Beri said to herself as the last crewmember got in the ship and buckled himself. She started the exit sequence and the port bay doors to the Ray Patroller slid open slowly. The cockpit canopy lowered and the Light Ripper darted out into deep space.

Chapter 3

Pieces of light mixed with particle matter around the outer atmosphere of Planet York III. The fragments bounced off each other and some managed to spin in place and oscillate every few moments. Suddenly a comet blasted through the atmosphere, causing the leftover particles to reactivate. One small particle began emitting a bright yellow light and doubling in size. As the particle moved nearer to Planet York III's outer atmosphere, it started gaining speed and heat. Nearby organisms tried to latch on to the speeding particle, but they were no match for its growing speed.

The ever-growing particle was now the size of a soccer ball, and it began to emit screaming sounds that were reminiscent of a boiling teakettle. As the ball continued to grow bigger and get closer to Planet York III, it morphed from a spherical shape into a more humanoid figure that was beginning to see, smell, and sense the atmosphere that it was quickly hurtling towards. The humanoid particle did know what was happening, and it certainly didn't like the ending to this journey that was about to transpire. It started to scream out of fear, pain, and ignorance.

A few hundred miles above Planet York III's surface, the being had its first thought.

"I don't want to die!"

And then it landed with a gigantic thud. The humanoid lay there, in excruciating pain from the plunge, but miraculously still alive.

A nearby farmer was awakened by the thud and grabbed a glow lamp and a static spear used for killing scavenger animals. He pulled back some tattered curtains and peered out of his bedroom window. His wife jumped out of bed from the sudden commotion and looked scared.

"What is it?" she asked.

He squinted, trying to adjust his eyes in the darkness. He could barely identify what appeared to be a small crater in the middle of his farm.

"I'm not sure, but you stay here," he said to his wife. "I'll go see." He was too poor to afford a night scanner, so he would have to investigate the odd scene the old-fashioned way.

The being, which was now the size of an adult human, began to scan its surroundings. It looked at its appendages, which were bright, clear, and white. It didn't feel much pain anymore. It looked down at the massive hole where it landed and saw pieces of light bouncing around it. The being stood up, wobbly at first. It could barely see over the edge of the top of the hole. A small, singular light was quickly heading toward it.

With amazing speed, the humanoid climbed out of the hole, trying not to be seen by the approaching intruder. As it cleared the initial hump of the crater, it noticed a few large stationary objects clustered not too far away. The creature ran as fast as it could to try to take cover.

The farmer saw the creature climb out of the hole and began to chase after it. He screamed and yelled, trying to scare the thing off. "Get off my land!" he yelled.

He noticed it was heading toward a grove of bush trees near the edge of his farm. The creature had a slight glow to its skin, making it easy for the farmer to see its sporadic movements in the dark. He wasn't too worried that the creature was dangerous anymore. It fled as soon as it was spotted. Now his main concern was saving his crops.

The creature darted back and forth wildly, trying to lose the strange light that was following behind it. It reached the cluster of trees and quickly ducked behind the biggest one. It turned around to see where the floating light was. While it gained a significant lead during the chase, the creature took a misstep backward and tumbled down a steep bank toward a lake. Branches, leaves, and mud were flying all over the place as the humanoid slid down into the bottom of a bank. There was something moving just at the bottom of its legs.

The creature stared into this motioning black liquid. As the waves began to slow, it began to get a clearer vision of itself. It had the face of a woman, with blue glowing eyes and short, jet-black hair. She wasn't sure what to think about her appearance. Curiously, she dipped her hand into the black liquid, causing ripples in it. Her reflection became distorted.

A sound suddenly came from behind her. She quickly stood up, ran to the bank, and flattened herself against the edge. She still had a slight glow radiating from her skin into the pool of motioning liquid. She knew she had to cover herself to minimize the light. She slid quietly along the bank wall away from the noise she had just heard.

As she moved down the bank, she saw a line of garments attached to a rope. The rope was attached to one of the trees' roots on the top of the bank and the other end was tied to a short pole in the mud. The creature noticed a dark garment that was close to her size. She grabbed it and pulled, noticing that it stretched a little. She tried to put it on a few times before getting it right. Her glow, thankfully, subsided.

The farmer, finally reaching the wooded area, began to walk on the edge of the bank looking for the intruder. He held his glow lamp in one hand and his spear in the other, ready at any moment for an attack. He thought he heard a noise at the far end of the lake so he walked over cautiously. No sounds could be heard. But he did see a faint glow in the lake, although it was much dimmer than that of the creature he was chasing. The creature had probably drowned, he thought.

Feeling his pursuit was a success, he turned around and headed home. After a few minutes, he exited the small forest and strolled across his land. As he approached his house, he could see a light hovering near a hole in the ground. He heard his wife's voice as he came closer.

"What was that thing?" she asked.

"Not sure, but I think it fell into the lake and drowned."

"At least you are safe," she said giving him a hug, "and everything is still here.

"Not everything," said the farmer. "I think it stole your bathing suit."

Officer John Vaggs, now wearing his off-duty garbs, sat slumped in his chair, depressed at the outcome of the night's events. He found himself on jail patrol duty, the lowest job for an enlisted man in this military regime. The only thing worse was being demoted, which he was fairly sure would be Captain Nammill's fate. The stone hallway where John was keeping watch was dimly lit, just enough light to keep his eyes from straining. He listened for a moment, trying to hear if any of the prisoners were awake. No sound existed, except for some light snoring.

John reached into his utility belt and pulled out his communicator. He turned the dial from his local channel to the broadcast channel. The radio crackled loudly, and he quickly lowered the volume. He held the device close to his ear and slouched in his chair.

"Current investigations are underway concerning the explosions in Ombrick," a mechanical voice said.

There was a pause with static.

"New developments," the voice continued. "Meteor activity spotted fifty miles north of Lyonne was reported approximately ten minutes ago."

"I wonder," John said under his breath.

Suddenly a cough from the cell directly behind his seat startled him. He dropped the communicator to the stone floor. The volume rose instantly with a loud cracking sound.

"A large crater was found in a farmer's yard, apparently caused by a meteor," the mechanical voice said echoing throughout the jail hallway. "Possible links to previous explosions in Ombrick are being investigated."

John hurriedly tried to grab the device but a bony, dry-skinned hand reached through the jail cell bars first. The device disappeared into the cell behind the officer's chair. John knelt on the stony floor trying to see who or what had taken his communicator. Through the dim light he recognized the professor. Dr. Nolan, barely able to sit up from the pounding pain in his head, had a surprising smile on his face. He turned the volume down, but left it just loud enough for John to hear. Dr. Nolan lifted the radio to his ear, his eyes full of life.

"Meteor activity is still persisting," the voice stated from the broadcast.

There was another static pause.

"A few citizens of Lyonne have reported a ghostly female figure wandering the streets. It is unclear whether this is related to the situations earlier reported."

John, beginning to get nervous, pleaded with Dr. Nolan. "Please, professor. Give me back the communicator."

Dr. Nolan's happiness paused for a moment. He tilted his head with question in his eyes, looking at the officer in front of him begging for the device. For the first time tonight, he noticed the face of the young officer. This face was very familiar.

"John?" he questioned with a soft voice.

John lowered his head. "Yes," he reluctantly affirmed.

"How could you?"

"Shhhh!" John pleaded, trying to calm the professor down. "You might wake the others!"

"I can't believe you would do this to me! After all I tried to do for you."

John couldn't say anything. He just looked down at the floor. He already felt guilty about his past. He didn't need more condemnation from the professor.

"You were my favorite student, John," Dr. Nolan said with a heavy heart, "And my brightest." He shook his head in disgust. They both sat there on the cold, smooth stone floor, starring at each other.

"You have to let me out," Dr. Nolan said, trying to stand up.

"Are you crazy? I'll be executed for releasing a prisoner."

"Not if you come with me. The greatest experiment in the history of this planet was successful. You can be a part of it, but you have to help me," Dr. Nolan said, trying to plead with his one-time student. "The scientist within you cannot resist this!"

John was speechless and dazed. His world was unraveling again. Just a few years ago he was enjoying his life, studying at Gobgin Technical University. He was a young, talented, smart man with so much potential. Then the invasion happened, and he chose to join the winning side of the war for his own survival. Now an old friend from his past was asking him to change sides once again, this time back to the side for which his heart truly longed.

"John," Dr. Nolan said quietly, limping toward the jail cell bars, "I created life in space!"

John was very familiar with the professor's lifelong goal. Dr. Nolan, Dr. Benni, and John, as a pupil, had spent many months in a laboratory trying to prove theories that this goal was even remotely achievable. He was shocked that Dr. Nolan had finally succeeded. John didn't know what to say or do. He stood up slowly.

"We have to find her, my baby, or she'll die," Dr. Nolan said, pleading with John. "You have to let me go."

Feeling as if an unseen force controlled his hand, John reached for his key ring and reluctantly unlocked the cell door. He lifted the latch and pushed the steel door up over his head. The old professor smiled, feeling the most relief he had felt in many years. He patted John on his right shoulder and smiled.

"Good job, son."

John felt a hollow pit in his stomach. He would surely be killed for this. They both stood there in the dimly lit stone hallway, each wondering how they had come to this point. Then John snapped out of the trance.

"We have to get out of here, quickly! Opening a cell is transmitted to headquarters," John said to the professor. "This way."

John pulled Dr. Nolan's arm as he led the tired and limping old man down the corridor. He needed to find a way out of the castle dungeons without passing any of the night patrol. It was a good thing he knew most of the patrol's routes. Unfortunately, he hadn't been in this part of the castle. Just as they neared the far end of the hallway, a familiar voice called out weakly.

"Vaggs."

John stopped abruptly.

"Captain?" John questioned turning toward the cell on his left.

There, to John's surprise, was Captain Nammill slumped in a cell, weak and bruised. The cell had a red light located above the steel door, marking the prisoner inside for termination. John leaned closer to peak into the cell. Dr. Nolan was getting suspicious and he tugged on John's uniform, a motion to leave.

"What are you doing in here?"

"Never mind," Nammill said. "Just be careful, kid. This regime doesn't take too kindly to traitors." He pushed an unknown device through the cell bars.

"Take this," he said weakly. "Call for help."

John bent over and picked up the device. It appeared to be some kind of radio but not one he'd seen on this planet before. It had an emblem with a yellow and black star within a red octagon. Dr. Nolan shook his head indicating that he didn't trust the captain.

"It might be a tracking device," Dr. Nolan whispered to John. He ignored the professor's warning and stuffed the device into his utility belt.

"What is it?" John asked, not sure if the captain would tell him the truth.

"Let's just say it's a direct line to some old friends of mine. Now get out of here. The blue hallway is the quickest way out."

John instinctively wanted to save his superior from bondage, but releasing a prisoner from a termination cell would sound the alarm. Not needing the jail keys anymore, he slid them into the captain's cell, hoping Nammill would free himself. Reluctantly John and the professor turned and left the jail corridor. John hadn't been in this area before so he had no choice but to follow the captain's suggestion. He made a direct path toward a hallway with dim blue lights lining the floor, pulling the professor behind.

Making a few moves to avoid the night patrol guards, the two escapees soon found themselves standing behind a wall next to the capital city's palace looking onto the main street. They could now hear the alarm sounding within the palace walls. Eventually the alarm would sound throughout the entire city once the guards discovered that John had escaped with Dr. Nolan.

"We need to find a hiding place," John said.

"We can go to Vara's house," the professor replied. "She gave me a key in case of emergencies."

Dr. Nolan pointed toward the direction of Vara's home. The two set off into the night, moving quickly, trying to stay in the dark corners of the city.

The female being from space had run a long way from her birthplace where she had her crash landing. She wasn't sure where she was going. She just kept moving away from the crazy being with the glowing stick. She didn't know that it had stopped chasing her hours ago.

She roamed the streets of this massive city, in the dark, unwillingly lighting her own path and leaving smatterings of floating light particles. She could hear an annoying noise from off in the distance repeating itself. The inhabitants of the city didn't seem to take kindly to her intrusion. The larger beings that spotted her yelled at her and many ran back into their dwellings, closing the entrances behind them. A few stood their ground, as if to try to frighten her away. The smaller beings just hid their faces. She tried to ignore these strange creatures and keep moving ahead.

From the side of one of the smaller dwellings, in a dimly lit alley, a cloaked alien emerged holding a few spoils from its last robbery. This species had the ability to change its smooth skin to match any color and texture it so desired, allowing it to hide extremely well. It stood upright like a human most of the time, walking on its clawed feet. But it typically ran on all six limbs for more speed. This particular male alien was four feet tall and stout. He was well known around these parts for his criminal activity. The locals called him Maco.

The glowing female didn't see Maco, but he definitely saw her. He was rather fascinated by the sight before him, this humanoid female, strolling through the largest city on the planet, glowing in the dark. Wearing nothing but a blue swimsuit, this female creature seemed to be headed in no particular direction, maybe because she didn't know where she was.

"She won't get far like that," Maco muttered to himself.

He decided to follow her cautiously. Not knowing what she was, he was careful to not alert her to his presence either. Maco quickly changed his skin to match every object he hid behind as he followed this glowing female through Lyonne. Then he stopped behind a stone fence near a house. A small group of night patrol guards were just ahead.

"This could get very interesting," he mumbled to himself as he ducked lower behind the fence and closed his outer eyelids for protection.

"Halt!" said the leader of the patrol guards to the glowing female. He held his right hand out in front of him trying to stop her motion.

Much to his surprise, she stopped in her tracks. She was not scared of the group of beings blocking her way, but she was more amazed that this group was actually talking to her. She could sense some danger so she proceeded carefully. She opened her mouth and spoke garble. The leader of the pack raised a weapon and pointed it at her face.

"Kneel on the ground and put your hands behind your head."

Maco, who understood the human language quiet well, was watching and listening intently. The glowing female, not sure what these words meant, covered her eyes. She peeked between two of her fingers to see what these beings would do next. She couldn't communicate with them and they didn't seem to care. Three more officers ran from behind one of the dwellings and positioned themselves behind her. She was surrounded and starting to feel scared. They were all pointing these thin, black metal sticks and grey cylinders at her. She didn't know what to do. She wanted someone to help her.

"I said get on the ground!" the leader yelled more intently. He motioned the group to move closer toward her.

Not far from the commotion, Dr. Nolan and John were zigzagging through the alleys of Lyonne. Dr. Nolan heard the yelling and instinctively knew that his creation was nearby and possibly in trouble. He stopped abruptly and peered around an abandoned house.

"She's over there!" he yelled to John who was still heading toward Vara's house. "We have to get her."

The professor darted into the alley next to them.

"No!" John said stopping his run. "They'll capture us, too!" He pivoted and changed his direction.

Dr. Nolan started running much faster now and John wasn't able to gain much ground. The professor finally came to one of the main city streets and stopped just before entering it. Moments later, John stopped directly behind him.

There, in the middle of the street, about one hundred yards away, was his creation, living and breathing.

"What is it?" John questioned softly.

There was no answer from the professor, because he wasn't sure himself. The glowing female was becoming very scared as the night patrol guards came closer to her from opposing sides. She put out her hands in either direction trying to signal them to stop, imitating the gesture one of the guards had done earlier. The look on her face was one of fright and anger. The guards crept closer. She closed her eyes, not knowing what would happen next. As she stood there, her hands began to glow brighter and brighter. Dr. Nolan was awed by his creation.

The guards, becoming wary of the creature's glowing hands, aimed their weapons to fire. Dr. Nolan, sensing what was about to happen, darted into the street.

"No! Leave her be!" he screamed.

The guards turned to look at Dr. Nolan and John standing just behind him in a dark alley. In a panic, one of the guards fired his weapon. The fracture rifle emitted a blue electric wave directly at the glowing female. She flinched and two balls of light flew from her hands at the guards. An explosion occurred, followed by a deafening sound like thunder, as the balls of light hit the ground, throwing most of the guards back off their feet.

Dust and rock flew everywhere and a strange fog emerged from the wake of the blast. All of the city's bright blue emergency lights turned on and a bellowing alarm sounded. The alarm was so loud that Dr. Nolan and John covered their ears. The glowing female collapsed to the ground.

"My baby!" the professor screamed as John tried to pull him back into the alley.

In the distance they could hear vehicles approaching and radios crackling. For the military of this regime and the guards on patrol, this explosion looked like an attack. Soon every soldier and mercenary would swarm this area and any person, alien, or anything else they didn't recognize as friendly would surely be destroyed.

"We have to go, professor!" John said fearing for both of their lives.

Amid the dust, fog, and falling rock, Maco saw his chance. He could use a power like this female humanoid on his side. Somehow he had to convince her. He got on all sixes and scrambled toward the fallen female. He shook her slumped body, trying to wake her up. She turned over to see him and she quickly started backing away. He didn't look like the other beings at all.

"I'm here to help," Maco said, knowing she didn't understand his words. He tried to make motions of friendliness with his four hands.

He held out one of his hands in a gesture of assistance. The female seemed to understand and grabbed his hand. Maco flipped her on top of his back and dropped on all six limbs. Maco was astonished by how light she was. He thought for a minute and decided to lower the glowing female back to the ground. Even if he could run, her glow would surely get them both caught before he could exit the city. There had to be another way.

As the dust and rock started to clear, some of the guards were beginning to stand up. A few could be heard relaying their location to the base. Military vehicles were turning onto the main street heading in their direction.

Maco jumped. The female looked at him with question in her eyes. He jumped again and then motioned for her to repeat. She jumped, quite a bit higher than he did. Maco realized his plan might work. He could see the guards and transports headed their way. A few of the closer guards were reloading their weapons. Maco jumped higher, and the glowing female repeated, this time leaping far above the tops of the houses. Maco stood there, looking up at her, hoping she would come back down.

Dr. Nolan, still struggling to release himself from John's grip, continued to call for the female being. John tried to pull the professor behind the nearest house, hoping they could hide there. Dr. Nolan kept trying to run into the commotion in the street. Just then, an arm wrapped around John's neck, choking him, and another covered his eyes. He lost sight of Dr. Nolan as he was pulled away into a dark alley, unable to see what was happening.

The armored vehicles came to a screeching halt just a few yards from Maco. He was completely surrounded by guards with guns aimed at his head and hovering battle vehicles with huge cannons. But Maco didn't care. He kept staring straight up. As one of the guards approached Maco to apprehend him, the female humanoid dropped out of the sky with a thud, creating a small crater in the dirt. The guard stumbled from the impact and fell to the ground. As quickly as she had fallen into the scene, the glowing female wrapped her arms around Maco and jumped again, this time with enough force to launch high into the night sky. A small light, not much bigger than a speck, was all that could be seen of her from the ground.

Chapter 4

John, barely able to breathe through the chokehold, could feel himself being dragged by a very strong person. Suddenly he heard a door close in front of him, and he felt complete darkness and cold surround him. The grip loosened, and the stranger dropped him onto a cold, slippery floor. John coughed, regaining his breath. The door opened again and John could see a large, muscular man dragging Dr. Nolan, who appeared to be unconscious. The man squeezed Dr. Nolan into the tiny room beside John and shut the heavy door behind him. John wasn't sure what was happening. He scanned the room quickly hoping for a way out, but the large man was blocking the only exit.

The man blocking the exit spoke to the other kidnapper. "The old man fought hard, didn't he?" Then he turned to John, "Hopefully you two didn't cause too much commotion. Otherwise, we are dead men."

John, sensing that these two men were not enemies, but not sure if they were friends either, said nothing. He could barely see the professor lying next to him.

The man who had dragged John into the small room took off his coat. He flung it onto John's head. The coat smelled of body odor and smoke. John reluctantly wrapped the coat around his back.

"That will keep you warm, weakling," he said. "My sister will shut off the power in a moment. Then the box will start to warm up."

"She should be released from the medical ward in a few minutes," the other man chimed in. "We just need to stay here till the morning. There are way too many alarms to go anywhere right now. Besides this freezer only unlocks from the outside."

Dr. Nolan groaned from exhaustion. The more muscular of the two men bent over and gently wrapped his coat around the professor. "Hopefully the crazy old man will sleep until dawn."

Outside the walls of the tiny room, shuffling feet and shouting could be heard. A few weapons fired. Screams from women and children echoed. John wondered what was happening outside in the city. He feared that the female humanoid was dead. He hoped she had managed to escape.

Suddenly there was a loud slam on the door to the tiny freezer room. It shook the box off of its base. The two men held out their hands to stabilize the freezer. It settled and the sound of a motorized vehicle leaving was all that they heard. They all relaxed.

"That was close," said one of the men.

"I hope our sister turns off that power soon. It's getting really cold in here now," said the other one, rubbing his arms. He could feel his fingers growing numb.

Then, as if she heard his prayer, the sound of electricity being disconnected reverberated through the entire box. Quickly the cold began to escape. John took off the coat and tossed it at the stranger standing over him.

"Thanks," he said.

"We are always willing to help Vara."

Then John realized these two men were Vara's older brothers, Wilson and Cakk. She must have called them and told them what had happened at Dr. Nolan's house. John hoped her brothers didn't remember that he was now one of the officers working for the military. These two would surely throw him out into the street to face his own demise. For now, he and the professor were safe, or so he thought.

"It's a good thing you're a friend of Vara's," Wilson, the older of the two brothers, said while putting his coat back on. "If it were my choice, I'd leave you outside to the wolves."

John could hear the anger in his voice. He decided to remain silent. Defending his actions would not be a good idea right now.

Cakk, the younger and more forgiving brother, said, "Calm down, Wilson. He hasn't killed anyone. John couldn't hurt an Udderlick."

"Well, he's responsible for killing someone just by working for Admiral Raynger," said Wilson in disagreement. "He's probably going to stab us in the back at any moment."

Wilson had always been the hot-tempered one. His tall and muscular build allowed him to be a bully, and he was used to getting his way. He never liked John Vaggs, especially after he became smitten with his sister.

"Vara still believes in him," Cakk said with a calming voice.

"She's naive," Wilson huffed.

He knelt down over John, his breath slightly warming John's head. Vaggs, who had been intently listening, turned to look up straight into Wilson's angry eyes. "You make one wrong move, Johnny, and I'll wring your neck myself."

Ty turned to his attention toward Beri. She was staring straight ahead, looking through the clear cockpit windows of the Light Ripper out into deep space. Ty put on his pilot's helmet and motioned toward Beri, but she didn't respond.

"Captain, we are nearing our destination."

"Huh?" Beri questioned seeming to snap out of a trance.

"Should we let them know we are approaching, so they don't shoot us out of the sky? They might actually let us dock."

"Oh, yeah, right," Beri said, taking off her helmet.

Her long, curly, brown hair fell out of her helmet and lay on her back. She nervously picked up the communicator sitting on the dashboard in front of her. Ty could see that she was unsure of herself being the leader of this mission. Beri wondered if the other agents could feel her nerves. She put the communicator close to her lips, guessing that she would receive the same message from the Ray Patroller.

"This is Captain Beri Onex aboard Light Ripper beta-seven-beta approaching Ray Patroller four-five-gamma-theta in QX Sector. We are on a reconnaissance mission. May we dock?"

There was a pause then a crackle on the radio.

"Nothing to report," said the voice again.

"As usual," Ty said sarcastically. "Next move, genius?"

This was Beri's first mission as a leader, and she knew this would go a long way in impressing her superiors back in the RY sector, maybe, possibly leading to apromotion. She had to be successful. Getting Ty to back her up would be a critical step. Beri whirled around in her seat to address the other passengers who were sitting quietly.

"Who has a datapad?" she asked in a commanding voice.

The other four agents took off their helmets and reached underneath their seats. Beri turned to Ty, who was now flying the spaceship.

"Officer Chu," she said. "Take a long, circular route toward the Ray Patroller and put the Light Ripper into stealth mode."

Ty was completely surprised by this command. He knew that putting a spaceship in stealth mode was a move intended for hostile territory. Just before he locked in the stealth mode setting, he asked Beri, "Are you sure about this?"

"Just do it, Ty," she said lowering her voice. "If this sector is compromised, we could be in real danger. There aren't that many of us in this ship to fight a war with aliens or pirates. I'd rather be safe than sorry."

"Found it!" Vince shouted, holding up his datapad.

"Junior Agent Filtreth. Research the time of the last communication from this sector that wasn't 'Nothing to report,'" Beri commanded.

"Senior Agent Jovic," she said. "Get me the data on the Sci-Fi Force squad in this sector, from the last ten years."

"Any particular filter on that data, ma'am?" Penn questioned.

"Ships, weapons, and personnel, mainly," she said. "And anything else you think I should know. She looked over to Hilton and bellowed, "Junior Agent Rrorr?"

Hilton stood up at attention, adjusting his goggles behind his short blond hair.

"Ready the manual weapons and check the ship's systems," Beri continued. "We might need evasive maneuvering capability. And Junior Agent Wenn, find out what you can about resources on the nearest planet."

The junior agents felt the sense of urgency and fear in her voice. They weren't quite sure why the atmosphere had changed, but it was obvious it had. Beri whirled back around in her seat to see a surprised Ty staring at her. He wasn't sure what to say.

"Head in that direction," Beri said, pointing at the cockpit glass. "Take a high-to-low route just in case they are tracking us."

"Are you going to call for back up?" Ty asked.

"Not until I'm certain we need their help."

Beri gazed through the glass, trying to catch a glimpse of the Ray Patroller. She and Ty could begin to see the massive space ship in the distance as they came closer. It hovered there with its docking lights still lit. There was no other activity in the vicinity. Even the tiny blinking lights, which had led them this way in the first place, had stopped. Beri was thinking about what they should do if they entered hostile territory with so few agents. She was trying to prepare herself for the unexpected.

"Ma'am!" Vince shouted, causing Beri to jump in her seat. "I found the last communication from this sector that wasn't 'Nothing to report.'"

"It was nine years ago," Vince said quietly, sounding unsure of his own words.

The entire crew was shocked. They all became nervous and a little scared for their lives. They stopped what they were doing, hoping that Beri would tell Ty to turn around and take them home. Beri looked at Ty, then out through the cockpit glass. They were nearing the giant spaceship, and soon they would be docking in its hull. Its black and grey covering created an ominous presence.

"Are they all dead?" Ty asked. He began to put the Light Ripper into landing mode, preparing to land this entire crew into a death trap.

The glowing female continued to fly straight up into the air. The wind she created by her speed blew through her short black hair. The cold temperature of the outer atmosphere did not affect her, but it was beginning to affect Maco. He was also beginning to feel weak from the lack of air at this height. He looked down at the city of Lyonne, which was not much larger than a coin on the planet's surface. He tapped the female on the back, hoping to get her attention, even though she seemed determined to fly straight into deep space. She looked down at Maco, noticing that he seemed to look weak. He motioned down.

Understanding Maco's communication, the female stopped her flight, and the two began to free-fall. Maco was beginning to feel sick. He pointed toward the mountains to the northeast of the city, trying to get this female humanoid to go there. She seemed to understand. The city of Lyonne was growing bigger by the second.

Then, seemingly with no effort, the female darted through the sky toward the direction of Maco's finger. She turned him over in her hands so that he could better guide her path. As they flew, Maco pointed out different things, saying what they were in human language. The female uttered some garble, trying to repeat what Maco was saying, some words sounding much better than others. As they neared the tallest mountains, Maco said something that the female understood as the word for "Home."

She slowed her flight and lowered her altitude, getting closer to the mountains and flying between the cliffs. Maco pointed toward a cave and she headed there. She landed on the ledge at the mouth of the cave with an abrupt halt, kicking up dust everywhere. She dropped Maco rather carelessly, and he collapsed to the ground. Maco sat for a few moments gathering his bearings. He shook his head and stood up trying to gain his balance. She rushed to him to make sure he wasn't hurt.

"I'm alright," he said, still feeling dizzy.

He looked at the female humanoid glowing in the dark looking worried. He stood up with her assistance and dusted himself off. He pointed to himself.

"Maco," he said, using the name the humans had given him. "You are?" he asked.

She pointed to herself, "Maco."

"No, no," he said grabbing her hand and pointed to himself. "Maco."

She paused. She understood what he was asking her. What did she call herself? The glowing female looked at Maco with a blank stare. He realized that either she didn't have a name or she didn't know her name. He decided to name her. Maco pointed her hand to herself.

"Altaira," he said giving her a female sounding name.

She nodded in approval and repeated, "Altaira." Then she pointed toward the cave. "Home," she said.

"Yes," agreed Maco, "Home."

The alien dropped onto all six limbs and entered the cave followed closely by Altaira, lighting the way in the tunnels.

The Ray Patroller's glass hangar doors slowly slid closed as the Light Ripper passed through. The small ship's landing thrusters kicked on and lowered the Light Ripper to the slick, steel black floor. The only motion within the hangar was the blue landing lights flashing periodically. Beri and Ty gazed out through the cockpit window. Beri was scared for herself and her crew. She couldn't let her voice portray her fear. She put on her helmet and shut her tan visor, partly because it was protocol and partly to conceal the expressions on her face. Her crewmembers awaited her next orders.

Beri turned around in her seat, "Penn, is there any data?"

"I've got tons of names, weapons, and a few ships, but all data is at least nine years old. There's been no change in the data over the last nine years. Nothing looks out of the ordinary from the older data," Jovic replied.

"Any reports of disease?"

Penn typed a few things quickly. "Not that I can see. Definitely not anything that could wipe out an entire crew of a thousand or more people."

"We should take a precautionary scan, just to be sure," Beri said, hoping someone would volunteer. As she suspected, no one did. "Senior Agent Jovic, are you up to the task?"

"Yes, ma'am," he said, nodding.

"While Senior Agent Jovic runs a biohazard scan, we will prepare for our next plan of action."

Penn flipped his helmet visor on and turned toward the back of the spaceship. He unlocked the Light Ripper's small equipment container and removed a large, two-handed device. The device was a yellow and silver-lined mechanism that was shaped like an oversized bazooka. It was heavy and awkward and not intended for small, quick tasks. Penn realized that he could be walking to his death, just by carrying such a weapon into this mysteriously empty hangar. Even so, he was willing to follow the orders from his captain.

Penn walked over to the back of the Light Ripper and nodded to Hilton, indicating he was ready to exit the ship. With a regretful motion, Hilton raised the air lock with the push of a button. Then he lowered the spaceship's rear door. The remaining Sci-Fi Force agents could hear Penn's heavy breathing as he plodded down the ramp. He disappeared around the ship's side.

"He'll be fine," Beri said to her remaining crewmembers, while removing her helmet. "We have to focus on the things we can control. Ty, once Penn returns and gives us the clear, we should split up into two groups of three. This ship is way too big for one team to cover."

"Vince and Hilton," Beri said looking directly at the two Junior Agents. "You two will come with me. We are going to get this Ray Patroller back online and operational. Our destination will be the control room."

"Ty," she said turning toward him, "Penn and Lilac will go with you to the bridge. If anyone is alive on this ship, they will be at the bridge."

Thinking about a potential ambush scenario, Ty asked, "What if the bridge is locked?"

"If the bridge is locked, hold your position until we get to the control room. From there we should be able to override the system and get you inside." Beri paused. "If any party is attacked, immediately relay to the other group and return to the Light Ripper."

The crew began to check their weapons, making sure the devices were ready for immediate action. Beri and Ty simultaneously put on their helmets and lowered their visors. The rest of the crew followed. Once they were ready, they stood there, each with a ready posture, staring through the air lock's glass barrier, awaiting their partner's return. Little did they know what dangers lay ahead.

BANG!

A booming sound of metal on metal resonated through the hangar. There was a slight tremor felt throughout the tiny ship. Beri glanced over at Ty to see his facial expression. It was full of fear. Then a sound of rumbling began, gradually getting louder. Whatever it was, it was heading toward the spaceship. Ty ran over to the cockpit to look out the windshield. The other members of the crew readied their weapons, aimed at the air lock. The device that Penn was carrying a few moments ago landed on the Light Ripper, causing Ty to fall back into the pilot's seat.

"Damn!" Ty said

"What did you see?"

Ty stood up out of the chair, his heavy breathing was audible through his helmet. “Open the air lock. Hurry!”

Beri wasn’t sure what Ty saw, but it was obvious by the fear in his voice that whatever was out there wasn’t friendly.

“Penn is coming back!” Ty yelled. “If we don’t open the air lock and let him in, he’ll die.”

“Captain?” Hilton asked, his hand already on the air lock release button.

Beri had a difficult decision to make. If she opened the air lock, she could expose the entire crew to a biohazard and kill them all, or she could possibly let in whatever it was that was coming toward them and risk fighting a small war inside this tiny spaceship. Neither of those choices was appealing. Her only other option was to leave Penn out there in the hangar to die.

“Hold your breath and open the lock,” she said. “Get ready to fight,” she commanded, raising her magnetic pulsar rapid-fire gun.

They all took a deep breath, and Hilton pressed the button. The sound of the air being released whistled through the tiny cabin. The crew kept their weapons aimed at different heights, preparing to shoot anything that didn’t look like Penn. The rumbling sound came closer and closer. A few of the hands on the weapons began to shake.

Beri leaned toward Ty and whispered, “Ty, what did you see?”

“Humans,” he paused, “Crazy, diseased, humans.”

Chapter 5

Penn stumbled and fell to the floor of the Light Ripper, trying to catch his breath. He turned and looked up at Beri.

"There are hundreds of them," Penn said reaching into his pocket for a weapon. "We're going to die!"

Just as he grabbed the gun, a wild, emaciated male human ran around the Light Ripper and snarled, saliva dripping from his mouth. Beri shot him in the head, his body crumpling onto the exit ramp. A few more humans, craving fresh meat, ran around the corner, attempting to get onto the spaceship. The barrage began.

The six-man crew began shooting blue, gray, and yellow rays from their guns. The sound of rifles, automatic weapons, and pistols firing was deafening. As they killed the invaders, the bodies were dragged out of the way by others, surely to be consumed. The small entrance to the Light Ripper worked in the crew's favor as most of the cannibals didn't make it past the first step.

Suddenly Beri's pistol stopped working. She glanced down at the meter on its side. "Power needed," she read. "Damn!" She yelled over to Hilton, "My gun is dead."

Hilton shouted back, "My gun is losing power, too. We have about forty, maybe fifty, more shots on the rifles. Then we are doomed."

Beri turned and looked out the cockpit glass. Hundreds more diseased people were running toward the ship. They had to get out of here or they would be overrun. Beri sat in the pilot's chair and fired the boosters. The jolt caused the crew to stumble. Ty and Penn fell backwards toward the pilot's seat. Hilton grabbed a steel railing to keep from falling.

"What are you doing?" Ty asked, continuing to shoot the invaders.

Without answering Beri put the Light Ripper into hover mode, the vehicle lifting five feet off of the steel hangar floor. As the last emaciated human was shot off of the loading ramp, Beri signaled to Hilton to close the ramp and the air lock. Once the lock closed, the crew took off their helmets, revealing a group of sweating, panting, tired Sci-Fi Force agents. Ty ran over to sit next to Beri and take the controls.

"Any injuries?" Beri asked. There were no answers, only heavy breathing. "Hilton, how long before the Light Ripper loses power?"

"Two, maybe three hours. Not long enough to go back home," he answered reluctantly.

Beri turned toward Ty and said, "We have to fly to the bridge."

Ty, not willing to question her commands at the moment, obeyed. As the Light Ripper exited the Ray Patroller, the cluster of crazed humans could be seen scampering to the far corners of the hangar. The hangar door opened and the tiny spaceship exited. Ty took a sharp right turn and headed toward the bridge. Beri turned around in her seat.

"How thick is this glass?" she asked, pointing at the cockpit window.

"Three feet, I think," Lilac chimed in. Understanding where Beri's thoughts were headed, she added, "Too thick for the weapons on this Light Ripper. The Ray Patroller's glass will be even thicker. You'll need an explosive."

Beri turned toward Hilton. "I think we've got a few," he replied. "Who's up for a spacewalk?"

"I'll go," Beri responded, not skipping a beat. She got up from her seat and proceeded to the rear of the ship. She opened the air lock and stepped onto the ramp. Hilton came behind her and closed the air lock. He pushed a small silver button, which the agents called the vacuum button. A mist filled the space between the spaceship's exit ramp and the air lock glass.

There were some whirring sounds and a laser shot toward Beri from the upper right corner of the enclosure. The laser made a burning sound as it traced the silhouette of the captain's body through the mist. After a few moments, the mist cleared and Beri stood there cloaked with a silver glowing blob surrounding her body. The blob was gelatinous and moved with ease. Hilton released the air lock. Beri stood there, her left hand out, waiting for the explosives.

"We are almost in position," Ty said over his shoulder, indicating the crew should be ready.

Lilac dug into one of the cabinets under Hilton's seat and emerged with two bronze-painted explosives. Each device, shaped like a semi-sphere, had a single red button on the top and eight metal claws on the bottom. Lilac turned one of the devices over onto its backside in her hand.

"How long for the delay?" she asked.

"Set them for two minutes," Beri replied.

Lilac did as she was instructed. Then she handed both the devices to Beri. Hilton closed the air lock again. Ty put the Light Ripper into hover mode, just a few yards from the Ray Patroller's main bridge. The glass encasing of the bridge was completely black. He squinted to see into the bridge but there wasn't enough light. He turned on the communicator in his helmet.

"Can you read me, Captain?" he asked.

"Perfect," Beri responded, with a thumbs up.

She opened the latch next to her. She reached inside and pulled out a propulsion pack and strapped it to her waist. Hilton lowered the ramp. Instantly Beri was sucked out of the ship, flying a few yards out into space. She quickly reached down and ignited the propulsion. As she flew past the tiny ship toward the bridge's glass, the Light Ripper slowly pulled away. Ty didn't want the explosion to destroy their only transportation home.

Beri neared the glass and put her covered hand on it. This space covering allowed temperature changes and some other human senses through. Her radio chirped.

"Captain," Ty called. "What exactly is the plan here?"

"To get inside this Ray Patroller and sound the distress signal," Beri replied. "I want to get some history files, too, but they might have been damaged."

"What are you going to do if those blood-sucking humans are inside?"

"I'm hoping they get sucked into deep space from the explosion."

Beri reached into her pack's holster and pulled out one of the devices. She placed it onto the glass, pushing hard and hoping to make an indentation. She pulled and pushed against the glass, and suddenly a small piece of the bridge's window cracked and floated away. The device glowed blue and began to dig its way into the glass. All of its claws were embedded as deep as they could go.

"One down," she said, giving Ty some indication that this crazy idea might work. She moved down a couple centimeters and began to dig in the other explosive. After a few tries, the device took hold and also dug itself into the glass. She took a breath.

"Here we go," Beri said as she pushed the red destruct button on each of the devices.

She ignited the propulsion pack again, but this time, nothing happened. The boosters just sputtered.

"Get out of there!" Ty yelled into the radio.

"The pack's not working!" Beri said, trying not to panic. "Hilton?"

Hilton, still aboard the Light Ripper, was remotely monitoring all the devices Beri had. He checked the status of those devices on his datapad. He didn't have good news.

"The pack wasn't charged before you left. I wanted to conserve it because we are low on fuel for the Light Ripper. It will fire up again in a few moments."

"How long is a few moments?" she asked, feeling she didn't want to know the answer.

"Two minutes," he said.

Altaira stumbled and fell on the hard rock of the cave. A few small, spherical shaped lights fell from her body and onto the tunnel floor. Maco turned back to help her. He steadied her as she stood up. Noticing her fatigue, he felt the need to comfort her.

"Almost there," he said.

They plodded along and Maco began to speak, "This is my home, the place of my kind for millions of years. We lived on this planet, cared for this planet, protected this planet long before the humans got here."

"First, they came in small bands, but we eliminated them before they could colonize," he continued. "Then they started to arrive in larger numbers. It became increasingly more difficult to destroy them all, so we started organizing into small groups specialized for eradication of the human kind."

Maco paused and turned to look at Altaira to see her facial expression. Only fatigue showed. He noticed that her glow was fading.

"We weren't sure why the humans wanted this planet. There are a billion others to choose from. Eventually we found out why. They wanted this," he said, jumping over a small stream of yellow sparkling liquid.

"Careful," he cautioned, "It's hot." Not completely understanding, Altaira dipped her hand into the stream.

"No!" shouted Maco fearing that his prize possession would be permanently injured or destroyed.

Altaira lifted her hand from the stream and let the liquid drip back down, unfazed by its heat. Steam and bubbles rose from the disturbance Altaira had created. Maco stared at her in amazement. The power she had was unfathomable. He couldn't afford to lose her for any reason. Her future with him could be legendary. All he had to do was keep her on his side.

"The humans wanted our life source. We have always lived off of this source and having them steal it would have destroyed us. The humans called it many things, but we call it honey. Once they realized where the honey was, the humans began to capture our kind and torture us for information. Shortly after that, the wars started. For centuries, humans and natives waged war, each declaring that they had a right to this planet. The outcome was a stalemate. That is until Admiral Raynger arrived."

The tone in Maco's voice became angrier. Altaira noticed, but she was too fatigued to respond.

"Admiral Raynger landed here with more powerful weapons and legions of men, willing to obey his orders," Maco said. "He slaughtered half of our population. He helped the humans win the war, and that is why he must die. He will not stop killing and torturing us until he finds the source of the honey."

Maco stopped talking as they came to an opening in the mountain. The cave opened up into a gigantic cavern containing a massive city. The entire cave was lit up by the honey as it snaked through many streams and rivers. The city, which was primarily made of rock, was filled with thousands of aliens that looked similar to Maco. As they walked closer to the city, Maco and Altaira stopped at the entrance that was blocked by a deep, wide river of honey. Maco signaled to a few of the aliens who were on the other side of the river. They chattered something in their native language and then a few more joined the group. They all began to rotate a gear system that was planted in stone. A small bridge slowly began to emerge from the rock.

Altaira, feeling extremely fatigued now and not wanting to wait for the bridge, picked up Maco and jumped over the river. She landed gracefully and set Maco down on the smooth black stone. The aliens, completely stunned by what they saw, didn't move. Maco chattered something toward them. He turned toward Altaira.

"Friends," he said.

As they walked forward, many of the aliens began to walk with them. It was like a small parade. A few of the aliens were making musical sounds through their noses. Some were even dancing. Others were pounding their hands and feet on the rocks. As they neared the middle of the city, Altaira saw a short, upside-down egg-shaped rock, surrounded by six light fixtures, and planted in the stone road. Maco separated himself from Altaira and stood in the rock.

"Here, I am king!" he said triumphantly raising his four hands.

Many of the aliens understood what Maco said and a celebration began. There was more dancing, louder singing, and small, bright green explosions erupted throughout the city's square. Altaira was amazed at Maco's acceptance by this nation. She stared in awe at the thousands of aliens who continued to chatter, scream, and jump at Maco's return.

Suddenly, Altaira collapsed. A few older aliens broke through the crowd and gathered the slumped Altaira onto a hammock of purple garments. They carried her away, parting the rambunctious crowd as they went.

Beri, floating motionless in space, stared at the blinking red lights and awaited her demise. The space around her was quiet and lonely, like an open grave. This was no way to die, she thought, and Beri was not about to give up so easily. She lifted up both her legs and planted her feet on the glass of the Ray Patroller. With one heave, she extended her legs, pushing herself away from the Ray Patroller at a snail's pace. She could only hope that by the time the devices detonated she was at least far enough away to avoid immediate disintegration.

"What is she doing?" Ty asked, spinning around in his pilot's chair to face Hilton.

Hilton, not looking up from his datapad, replied, "She's buying time."

"But if she goes too far, we won't be able to save her!" said a worried Lilac.

Ty whirled back around in the chair and watched Beri float slowly farther away. "Any ideas?"

Hilton looked up from the datapad. "All we can do is hope. Her only chance is firing up the boosters before it's too late."

"Couldn't we go after her?" asked Penn, exasperated.

"We could, but we'd risk all of us dying before we reached a refueling port," Ty said. "We need to stay put until the situation resolves itself."

All of the agents wondered what would happen next. Ty continued to watch as Beri became smaller and smaller. Without warning, an explosion sprayed tons of glass and metal shards from the middle of the two bright blue spheres. The initial flash was temporarily blinding. The agents turned their heads away from the blast. As soon as the light faded, Ty looked back, scanning the area for Beri. He didn't see anything. "Hilton?"

Hilton looked at his datapad and pushed a few buttons on the interface. "She's alive, but I'm not sure where. Give me a few seconds."

"She's a genius!" Hilton said excitedly. "She's heading toward the planet below. She's using the gravity to help conserve the boosters' energy."

"Will she survive the landing?" Penn asked.

"If her space covering doesn't burn up in the atmosphere and the boosters have enough left in them, she's got a chance."

"There aren't any space cannons below, so she doesn't have to worry about that," Lilac said.

"How do you know that?" asked Hilton.

"Track her coordinates," Ty interrupted, putting the Light Ripper back into normal mode. "We'll worry about her later. We've still got to get the data from this Ray Patroller."

"I'm losing her connection, though," Hilton responded. "Soon she'll be too far away for a reading."

"Then we'll have to hurry."

Ty flew cautiously toward the open hole in the Ray Patroller's front glass. As they came closer, the pieces of debris waned, indicating that the Ray Patroller's bridge had reached equilibrium with open space. Ty placed the Light Ripper back into hover mode. Hilton was still staring at his datapad.

"Who's going in?" Ty asked turning toward the other agents. It was obvious that he was staying put. Since Ty was next in command, the other agents had a decision to make. They all looked at each other, hoping someone would volunteer. Hilton continued to look at his datapad, trying to appear busy.

"Ok, then," Ty said, liking his newfound power, "Vince, you're next."

Reluctantly Vince walked over toward the airlock's glass. Hilton pressed the button and Vince stepped inside. The same mist covered his body, and the encasing laser followed. He reached into the cabinets on his left and grabbed another propulsion pack. He looked at Hilton.

"Is this one charged?" he asked, hoping for a better answer than the one given to his fallen captain.

"Yes, but you still don't have a lot of time. Use it sparingly."

"Exactly," Ty interrupted. "So hurry up and get in there. You have two goals. Sound the distress signal and get the history files."

Vince nodded and Hilton opened the ramp. The vacuum sucked Vince out into space and immediately he fired up the boosters. He flew over toward the gigantic hole in the Ray Patroller. Once he was at the opening, he paused. He checked his communicator.

"I'm going in," he relayed to the agents aboard the Light Ripper.

Cautiously, Vince entered the unlit bridge of the Ray Patroller. The lights from the Light Ripper outside helped illuminate the large room. The control room of this massive ship was unusually messy. There were overturned chairs and desks, weapons laying carelessly on the floor, and no people anywhere in sight. Not even any dead bodies. Some of the chaos was apparently from the explosion, but it didn't look like this area of the ship had been disturbed in a long time. Vince could also smell a rancid odor within the bridge. He proceeded toward the admiral's commanding chair, located at the center of the bridge behind the control desk. There would be a distress signal lever inside. As he neared the chair, he noticed that it was facing backward, toward the bridge entrance into the rest of the ship.

"You okay in there?" Penn questioned over the communicator.

"Good so far." He reached out and turned the admiral's chair around. "Gah!" he gasped.

In front of Vince, slumped in the admiral's chair, was a human skeleton loosely covered in a tattered Sci-Fi Force uniform, clutching a pistol in its left hand.

"What's going on?" Ty asked through the radio.

"Admiral Raynger is dead."

Chapter 6

"Where are you, Hilton?" Beri thought to herself as she floated closer to Planet York III. "How long does it take to get data?"

She could feel herself being pulled in toward the planet below a little faster as each moment passed. She turned her head to face where she was going. Beri could barely see the planet below. Its dusty orange color reminded her of her home planet. The heat of the planet's atmosphere was beginning to fill her spacesuit. The warmth was a nice feeling, but the reality of the forthcoming situation was not. She tried the propulsion pack again, testing its strength. It sputtered and fired for a short moment, allowing her to turn completely toward the planet below. She decided to save any energy left in the boosters. If there was enough energy, she could use the boosters to slow her fall like a parachute. Little did the captain know that a creature had passed a very similar route just a few hours before. However, Beri would not share the same good fate. There was a beep and chatter from her radio.

"Ty?" Beri asked, feeling hopeful.

"Who is this?" an unfamiliar voice asked.

Beri was shocked. Either someone had deciphered her communication with the Light Ripper or there were other Sci-Fi Force agents on the same channel.

"This is Captain Onex of the RY Sector," she replied in a stern voice. "You?"

There was a pause and static. Whoever this was, they had no intent to respond.

Beri didn't have much time. She could only hope that the others were on the same channel and hearing this conversation. She repeated her question, "You are?"

"We see you, Captain," interrupted a familiar voice. "We are heading your way. Hold on."

"Thank goodness, Hilton," Beri said with a sigh. "But please hurry. This suit is getting hot and I'm picking up speed."

Aboard the Light Ripper the agents were ecstatic that their leader had not fallen yet. Ty raised the ship's energy for one last big maneuver. He would have to zoom toward the planet at an alarming rate to match Beri's gravitational pull and conserve enough energy to land. It's a good thing he was a well-trained pilot. Ty put the Light Ripper into a nosedive.

"Brace yourselves, everybody," he said. "Hilton, ready the ramp."

Hilton, leaning on the seat at the back of the ship, pressed the button to unlock the ramp. He looked down at his datapad, checking the Light Ripper's energy level. He noticed something odd.

"Officer Chu, there are two communicators below," Hilton said.

"What?! Who is the other?" Ty asked, not turning to look back.

"I don't know. And I'm not sure which one is Captain Onex. We are falling so fast that both are approaching us at an alarming speed."

This new realization was confusing and disheartening. The Light Ripper was in a dive, potentially heading toward the wrong signal, or even worse, a rogue signal. The other agents looked toward Ty, wondering if he would say something.

"I have an idea," Lilac chimed in. She pressed her communicator, "Captain, we need you to fire your boosters in a parallel path to the planet. Can you do that?"

"Yes," Beri responded in a cautious tone. "But hurry up. It's starting to get hot out here!"

They all awaited confirmation from Hilton. Hopefully the change in direction would indicate which of the two signals was coming from Beri. Ty continued on his course, hoping their initial guess was right.

"There she is," Hilton said loudly looking at the datapad. "Continue your present course."

"Great work, Lilac," Ty said. He raised the Light Ripper's speed, hoping he would have enough energy to finish the mission. The last thing he wanted was for these young agents to hear their captain burning alive in the atmosphere of Planet York III.

"It's getting bright," Ty said toward Hilton. "Let me know when she's close."

The outer layers of Planet York III were beginning to burn the sides of the Light Ripper. The cabin of the tiny spaceship was filled with orange light from the atmospheric gasses and minerals. The agents were getting nervous. There was still no sign of the captain other than a little blue dot on Hilton's datapad. Suddenly, something rather large hit the dashboard of the Light Ripper.

"Whoa!" Ty said, jerking back in his seat. "Hilton! What the hell just happened?"

Hilton had misjudged the paths of the two objects. He quickly pushed the button to lower the ramp.

"Captain?" Ty and Lilac said simultaneously.

There was no response. The agents were silently awaiting something, anything.

"Hilton!" Ty yelled. "Where is she?"

"Rotate the ship and kill the engines," Hilton said.

Not having any other indication that Hilton was correct, Ty had no choice but to do what he suggested. He killed the engines and flipped the ship around. The quick maneuver threw Hilton to the floor of the ship and knocked the other crewmembers out of their seats. They all stood up.

Penn and Vince were looking out the front of the ship into the orange dust, and Hilton and Lilac were peering out of the back toward the ramp. Then they saw Beri seemingly floating, lifeless, toward the back of the Light Ripper. Her body eased into the tiny spaceship and thudded against the airlock glass. The inside of the spaceship felt empty, cold, lonely, and solemn. Hilton closed the ramp and sat down hard on the Light Ripper's floor. Everyone, except Ty, turned to look at the captain, crumpled against the glass. No one said anything.

The door to the small freezer cracked open. A female hand reached around the opening and a soft voice spoke.

"Wilson? Cakk?" Vara asked.

"Hey, Sis," Cakk responded. "Has the confusion died down?"

Vara pulled the door open to reveal the four men squeezed in the little freezer room. Wilson and Cakk were standing over John and a slumped and groggy Dr. Nolan. Dr. Nolan's eyes cracked open as he was awoken by the voices.

"I think we are OK to move. We just have to be quiet," Vara whispered.

"Come on," Wilson said sternly.

He lifted John roughly off of the dirty floor. Cakk pulled the professor up gently, allowing the old man to regain some balance.

"Where is she?" Dr. Nolan asked.

Vara could barely see Dr. Nolan's worried face in the very early dawn sky. She could hear his tired, broken voice. Vara wasn't sure whom he was referring to. She assumed he was referring to her.

"I'm right here, professor," she affirmed.

Dr. Nolan shook his head indicating that Vara didn't understand.

Cakk pointed. "This way," he said, softly leading the professor.

Wilson shoved John out of his way and began to follow his brother. John stumbled and stopped right in front of Vara. She looked tired and beaten. Her head was wrapped with medical gauze. He could smell her fragrance mingled with smoke on her clothing. Vara looked into his eyes and paused for a moment, waiting for John to say something. She still looked beautiful to him, standing there in a modest thin shirt and a long, flowing skirt. John motioned to speak, but he decided against it.

"We should hurry," she said, closing the freezer door behind him.

As Vara left to follow her brothers and the professor, John noticed something out of the corner of his eye. There was a paper object attached to the outside of the freezer room. He ripped it off, folded it, and stuffed it into his pocket. He hoped he would have better light to see it later. He quickly jogged after the others.

As the group covertly knifed through vacant houses, Dr. Nolan kept mumbling to himself. He appeared slightly delusional, but John knew the reasons for his discomfort. They eventually reached Vara's house, and they entered through the back door as quietly as they could. Wilson and Cakk went straight into her kitchen, looking for something to eat. Dr. Nolan plopped down on the floor and wept softly. Vara consoled him, still not sure what he was mumbling.

John stood by the door, not sure what he should do next. He pulled from his pocket the pamphlet that had been attached to the freezer door.

There she was, the creature Dr. Nolan created. Her face was plastered on this pamphlet with a warning sign. Her short, jet black hair, her light blue eyes, and her face full of fear were not what one would expect to see on a warning sign. John knelt down and handed it to the professor. He looked up at the picture and smiled a small grin.

He read, "Unarmed but extremely dangerous. Reward for capture or destruction. Permission to kill on sight." His smile grew even wider.

"She's so powerful," he said with glee. "Even that nasty Admiral Raynger is afraid of her."

He turned the flap over to read further, "Creature appears human in nature. Black hair. Clear, radiant skin. Creature can fly and propel objects from hands. Unsure of her weaknesses, so use caution. Leaves trail of disappearing lights."

Dr. Nolan looked up at Vara and John with worry in his eyes.

"She's dying! We have to help her," he said, standing up clumsily, dropping the paper to the floor. "She's dying," he repeated.

Vara and John helped Dr. Nolan get to his feet. He began to pace around the room. Vara, still looking confused, glanced over at John. John showed her the bounty notice. She looked at it for a few moments and then she understood.

"It worked?" she asked in disbelief.

John nodded and smiled.

Vara knew the background information about the professor's experiments. She knew that he had struggled for years trying to do something that many of the brightest minds thought impossible. John and other fellow students had also spent many long nights in the laboratory with Dr. Nolan trying to help him achieve his goal. Now, he had finally done it, even if only as a byproduct of an accident. Vara began to smile, too. She turned and hugged John.

"That didn't take long," Cakk said as he re-entered the room.

Embarrassed by her sudden display of affection, she loosened her grasp.

The professor broke his silence. "We have to get back to the house."

Dr. Nolan began to head toward the front door of Vara's house. Cakk stepped in front of the door, still stuffing some food in his mouth. He crossed his arms and shook his head.

"You can't leave!" he said through a mouth stuffed with food. "They are looking for us."

"But…" Dr. Nolan paused, feeling as if no one understood the gravity of the situation.

"She might not even be alive," Wilson said, entering the room.

Dr. Nolan angrily responded, "She is alive!"

Vara raced over to the professor to calm him down. "Wilson and Cakk will find what you need. For now you should to stay here and rest."

Wilson looked at Cakk with disgust. "Now that's my idea of an early morning party. Digging through a pile of burnt straw, wood, and clay.

The Light Ripper softly landed, sputtering now that it had lost the last of its power. The ship touched ground on what seemed to be a farm plot. The early morning dew glistened on its body. There was no obvious motion anywhere near the small spaceship. The Sci-Fi Force agents left inside were defeated and exhausted. Their fallen crewmember's body still lay in the space between the ramp and the ship's body. No one wanted to open the airlock. Opening the airlock would bring the reality of Beri's death closer to them. Even Ty hung his head in his pilot's seat.

Suddenly there was a tapping on the ship's hull from the outside. Ty jumped out of his seat and drew his pistol. The tapping sounded again. Ty looked at Hilton, who also heard the noise.

"Are you picking up anything unusual?" Ty asked Hilton.

Hilton shook his head, looking at his datapad.

"Then lower the ramp," he commanded.

"But what about Beri?" Lilac asked.

Ty ignored Lilac's question. Hilton lowered the ramp slowly. Beri's body slid down, resting on the ground amidst some crops. An older man peeked cautiously around the corner, looking into the ship. He looked at the five agents and then at the body.

"You are the second thing to land in my farm today," he said, sounding somewhat perturbed. "This is a farm, not a graveyard."

Another human, a slightly younger woman, peeked around the other side of the spaceship. She didn't say anything but just stared at the crew inside.

"Do you mind moving this thing? You are killing my livelihood," the man said, tapping the hull again with a long stick that glowed at the end.

Ty lowered his weapon, no longer feeling threatened. "We would, but we are out of power," he said, hoping the old farmer would have some sympathy.

"Honey," his wife interrupted, "This one's alive."

She knelt on the ground near Beri.

"What?" Hilton exclaimed. Not thinking, he pressed the airlock button.

"No!" Ty said, but it was too late. The airlock was already released. He and the other agents held their breath. They stared, waiting for Hilton to collapse from lack of oxygen or some poisonous atmospheric gas, but he didn't. They all breathed slowly as they watched Hilton release Beri from her spacesuit. The suit disintegrated into the air. The atmosphere on this planet was apparently safe for humans to breathe. They all stood up slowly, and Ty was the first to exit the ship.

"You were lucky. You could have killed us all," Ty said angrily.

"She needs medical attention," the farmer's wife said. "I have some things in the house."

The man didn't like the idea of inviting strangers into his house. The expression on his face was of discontent, but he wasn't arguing with this wife. He motioned by pointing with his long, glowing stick toward a small house in the distance. As the agents looked where the man was pointing, they could see the reddish sun peering over a mountain range. Ty knew that soon, someone would be here to find them. Spaceships didn't just land on planets without political maneuvering and logistics. Landing without warning usually meant hostility.

Ty turned to the group. "Get your stuff and let's go."

The old man picked up the slumping Beri and the agents ran back into the ship to retrieve their supplies and weapons. They exited the Light Ripper wearing backpacks and holding their datapads. They all had at least two weapons strapped to their waist, some strapped across their backs. Hilton pushed a few buttons on his datapad and the Light Ripper's ramp closed. The woman led the group toward her house, walking briskly. Off to the left, Ty noticed a huge crater in the middle of the man's farm.

Not expecting the man to answer, Ty asked, "Do you normally have meteor activity in this sector?"

The old man laughed. "That was no meteor."

The sun's early morning rays cast a red glare into the room where Altaira slept. She opened her eyes slowly to see a small room with smooth, gray rock as the walls. She sat up on the floor, looking for some sign of life. There was no motion, no noise, no sign of anything. There wasn't even an exit. Altaira was not scared, but rather curious, considering the commotion that happened earlier when she and Maco had returned to his home. She stood up, only to fall down again. Her body was still very weak. She noticed a dark purple garment wrapped around her neck, the length almost covering her entire body. It was draped around her loosely. She ran her hands over the garment. It was flowing, light, and smooth.

Suddenly a door, not easily noticeable in the wall farthest from her, opened. Maco and a few other aliens entered. They walked over to her, one of them holding out small pieces of something toward her face. The others hovered close, inspecting her.

"Are you hungry?" Maco asked, indicating that the small things were some type of food.

"No," Altaira said with little emotion.

The aliens turned toward Maco wondering what to do next for her. Maco chattered something and they quickly left the room. Maco strolled over toward Altaira, who was still sitting on the stone floor.

"How are you feeling? Any stronger?"

"Better," she said. She pointed toward the purple robe. "This garment..."

"Consider it a gift. Purple is a color of power. It belongs with you.

"Come," Maco urged, taking her hand. "We need to prepare."

Altaira stood up, a little dizzy at first.

"Prepare for what?" she asked.

Maco did not answer. Altaira gathered herself and followed Maco out of the tiny room. The two strolled down a maze of dimly lit rock corridors and tunnels.

Altaira, constantly surveying her surroundings, managed to keep up with Maco. Soon they emerged on a balcony of some sort, looking down into the open city. Below were many aliens, all attending to various tasks. They all looked very stressed, busy, and determined. The ones that caught Altaira's eye were directly below her practicing a type of fighting. They had staffs, some longer than others, some thicker than others, and they were attempting to hit each other with them. It was some sort of training session.

"Are you interested in learning?" Maco asked, sensing Altaira's curiosity.

She nodded and leaped from the balcony into the midst of the aliens below. She pounded into the rock, creating a small dent in the floor. Immediately she was whacked across the head by one of the staffs. She collapsed onto the hard stone floor. The aliens all paused, staring at her, startled by her sudden entrance. She sat up holding her head where the blow had connected. She gazed up at Maco.

"Here," he said, throwing a stick from above.

Altaira stood up quickly, reached out her other hand, and caught the long staff. It was slightly heavy and it shone with a golden coating. It was one of the longer staffs, and Altaira felt some energy when holding it. She smiled, feeling that she was truly ready now. Placing it next to her, she looked at the alien closest to her and motioned for him to try to attack her. Not sure how to proceed, the alien approached cautiously. It swung the staff in an overhead motion and Altaira quickly blocked it, knocking the staff from the alien's grasp.

"Good!" Maco said, who approached Altaira from behind. "You learn quickly. However, that won't be good enough tonight. You need more practice."

"What happens tonight?" Altaira asked.

"We go to war."

Chapter 7

Ty paced back and forth through the tiny living room, his short black hair flipping across his face with every turn. Junior Agents Vince, Hilton, and Lilac tried to ignore his distress. Hilton reached into his backpack and pulled out various devices and batteries, sprawling them across the old wooden floor. He fumbled through many different cords and wires. He was obviously still affected by the recent events. Vince, his head lowered, continued to type on his datapad, carefully documenting the group's actions, just in case he was questioned later. A little boy sat in an old wooden chair staring at Ty, his eyes full of excitement and curiosity. He was fascinated by the crewmembers in his parents' house with all of their gadgets and weapons. Lilac helplessly watched Ty pacing. She felt sorry for him so she decided to break the awkwardness.

"Officer Chu," she said, quietly at first. "What are we going to do about the Light Ripper?"

Ty stopped abruptly in his steps. He was surprised by her question. "I hadn't thought about it yet."

"I'm sure the local law enforcement will be here any minute to inspect the landing," Lilac said. "We can't all find places to hide in this little house."

She had a point. Their unauthorized entry onto this planet would surely be grounds for arrest. Without being able to contact the home base, they could spend a good part of their lives here imprisoned. That was not an option. Ty turned to Hilton.

"Hilton, how long before the Light Ripper has enough energy to fly?"

"Fly?" Hilton laughed, not even looking up from his mess of wires and devices. "Without a charging station, it will have to charge from natural sources. Unfortunately our closest station is surrounded by cannibals."

"What natural sources?"

"The sun, of course. But the sun's energy is weak in this sector. It will take some time."

"How long, Hilton?"

"About five days...and that's assuming that there's at least eleven hours of sunlight every day."

"How long before the weapons are fully charged?" Vince interrupted, sensing the eminent danger.

"That's what I'm working on now, guys," Hilton replied, exasperated by all the questions.

The farmer's wife emerged from the bedroom with a smile on her face. She wiped her hands in a light blue towel and walked over toward Ty.

"She's going to be alright," she said.

Ty and the agents were relieved. The farmer's wife patted Ty on the shoulder and walked to the kitchen to prepare a meal for the crewmembers. The farmer emerged from the rear of the house, followed closely by Penn. He shook the old man's hand and the farmer headed out the front door. Ty rushed over to Penn.

"How did it go in there?" he asked, hoping for good news.

"Surprisingly good, sir," Penn said, smiling. "She'll be much better in a few hours."

"We might not have a few hours. At any moment the local law enforcement could walk in an arrest all of us."

"I think you will be okay," the farmer's wife said, sneaking into their conversation from behind. "Please come into the kitchen and have some breakfast."

She placed a warm, friendly hand on Ty's broad shoulder. He had a flashback to an image of his mother. Her warmth and love made all of his fears go away. He hadn't seen his mother since the day he joined Sci-Fi Force, about five years ago.

Vince, Lilac, and Penn walked toward the kitchen seemingly without much concern about the local police showing up and having them thrown into a prison for a few years. Hilton remained on the floor, swimming in a tangle of wires. Suddenly there was an electric shock and a loud buzzing sounded from one of the long-range radios. Hilton jumped back.

"Hello?" questioned a male voice.

Ty turned around and glanced at Hilton. The two stared at each other, not sure what to say to the strange voice.

"Hello?" questioned the voice again. "Anybody there?"

The other three agents turned around to listen to the impending conversation. Ty slowly approached the radio and cleared his voice.

"This is Officer Ty Chu of the RY Sector," he said, praying he wasn't giving away too much information.

"Who are you?" Hilton interrupted.

There was a long pause. The group knew that this wasn't another Sci-Fi Force faction. Whoever this was, they had somehow gotten Sci-Fi Force equipment and learned how to break their encryption. It would be only a matter of time before either party could trace the other. They awaited the response, nervously.

John and Vara sat opposite each other at the tiny, circular dining room table. They both stared at the communicator in the center of the table. They looked into each other's eyes, then back at the device. Neither could decide what to say next. Fortunately, they didn't have to. The radio crackled.

"State your rank," the voice said.

John paused before answering, "I have no rank."

Vara wasn't sure if that was a good idea, but she said nothing. This device seemed to have a mind of its own. It just mysteriously turned itself on and began communicating with them. The static interference was so bad that neither Vara nor John could tell if the opposing party was man or machine.

"Are you friend or foe?" the voice asked.

They were playing a very good strategy game. Neither side wanted to reveal too much information for fear it would cost them their lives.

"Depends," Jonathan said, glancing at Vara for approval. "Which are you?"

"We have no enemies on this planet," the voice responded.

This was surprising news to Vara and John. Everyone on Planet York III had an enemy. The aliens hated the humans. The humans hated the aliens. Admiral Raynger's men hated the natives and the natives hated Admiral Raynger. Everyone hated the mercenaries and bounty hunters, and the hired killers hated each other. This stranger was obviously lying. It was time for the next move.

"How did you get a communicator for this radio signal?" the voice asked.

That was a question with a potentially revealing answer. Vara shook her head, indicating that telling this person that Captain Nammill had given away the communicator might not be a wise move. Not only might that information result in a swift death for Nammill, but it might also reveal their location and identity. John agreed, especially since he wasn't sure that this stranger was the person Nammill intended for him to contact.

"I found it," John lied. "Where did you get your radio?"

"From the factory that makes them."

John was beginning to get nervous. If his signal was being tracked, Admiral Raynger's soldiers would be storming Vara's house in seconds. The conversation had already taken too long. He had to make a move. He picked up the communicator and threw it on the floor.

"Do you have any...?" began the voice.

Before the question could be finished, John stomped on the communicator. It crackled and snapped under the weight of his foot, sending a few small metal pieces flying into the air. Vara stood up, somewhat surprised.

"They're tracking us," John said. "Nammill is a traitor. We have to get out of here now!"

Vara quickly understood and turned around to get Dr. Nolan.

"Professor?" she called.

There was no answer.

"Hilton?" Ty asked.

"I got a trace, sir," he replied. "It's coming from about twenty-five kilometers from here."

"We'd better get moving. There's not much time," Ty commanded, looking at the other agents. "If there are other agents here, rogue or not, they are our only chance of survival."

"What about Captain Onex?" Vince asked, sounding concerned.

"She'll be okay with us," the farmer's wife chimed in.

Ty nodded and smiled by her warmth and generosity. He and the rest of the crew began to load up their backpacks. He signaled the others to follow him. He threw his backpack over his shoulders and headed toward the door, his pistol strapped to his hip. Lilac, Penn, Vince, and Hilton all looked at each other, not sure if Ty's latest move was the right one. However, at this point they couldn't risk splitting up the group. Penn turned to the farmer's wife.

"Here," he said handing her some small objects she didn't recognize. "Give her these in a few hours. They will make her feel better."

"Let's go!" Ty said, getting louder as he opened the door.

All of the agents grabbed their belongings. Hilton was the last one to pack his mess. They each solemnly glanced at the closed bedroom door as they packed their stuff and headed outside the little house, once again wondering if they would see their captain again. Ty could see the old farmer in the distance working his crops.

He pulled out a scanner and surveyed the land. Off in the distance behind the Light Ripper, he noticed a small grove of trees positioned near the base of a few large mountain peaks.

"Hilton, is that our mark?" he asked pointing to the trees.

Hilton pulled out his datapad. He pressed a button and nodded affirmatively. Ty turned to the farmer's wife and thanked her again. He began jogging toward their first destination, his hands grasping the straps of his backpack. The other agents followed behind him.

Penn took a moment to thank her again, too. "You were a great help to us, and we thank you. Take good care of our leader. And if anyone asks, we were never here."

She was not quite sure what he meant or why he said that. The farmer's wife could see Hilton separate from the group and stop near their spaceship. He attached something to it that she couldn't clearly see. He then began to follow the rest of the agents toward the trees. Suddenly a bright yellow light flashed in the place of the spaceship, and a cloud of dust and smoke arose from the location. There was no audible sound. After a few minutes, the dust cleared and the spaceship was gone. The farmer's wife could barely see the last of the agents disappearing into the grove of trees.

"Professor?" Vara screamed. "Professor!"

She frantically ran to the bedroom in the back of the house. John quickly followed her into the tiny room. They both froze. The small window just above the twin bed was open. A slight, cool breeze flowed through the room. Immediately the two were filled with their greatest fear. Dr. Nolan had left.

"He's gone," John said quietly.

"But where?" Vara questioned, still staring at the window.

"He went home," John said, snapping his fingers. "He probably went to help Cakk and Wilson. He doesn't think they'll be able to find the pieces he needs to save his creation."

"But if he's caught, they'll arrest him again! We have to find him and bring him back. I don't think he can handle any more trauma."

Vara was worried. Her facial expression showed her fear. John wasn't too thrilled to perform a search for a crazy, frantic, old man in broad daylight, especially considering the entire army might be looking for them. But leaving the professor out to meet his demise wouldn't settle well with either one of them, especially Vara. John didn't want to see her upset anymore.

"Let's go," he said. "We are going to have to walk to Ombrick."

Vara grabbed John's hand, "But what if they catch us?"

"That just a risk we are going to have to take. C'mon, Vara. We have to save the professor!"

Vara wasn't going to argue. She didn't want anything bad to happen to them. All she could hope was that they could accomplish this impossible task together. John turned to exit the bedroom with Vara still clutching his hand. She let go, hoping that it wouldn't be the last time.

John grabbed his pistol and strapped it to his waist. He flung open the front door with Vara a few feet close behind. To John's surprise, he saw a familiar face.

"We meet again," said the alien mercenary. "Only this time I'm arresting you!"

The alien pointed his pistol directly in John's face. The alien's rancid breath filled John's nose and mouth, making him cough. Two men swiftly approached Vara from behind and tightly grabbed both of her arms. Vara twisted her body, trying to free herself, but it was useless. John stared into the black chamber of the weapon, hoping the alien wouldn't immediately kill him. He was trying to figure a clever way to get out of this situation. Then he heard another familiar voice.

"It's amazing what people will do to save themselves. Isn't it, Officer Vaggs?" Nammill asked.

Nammill strolled confidently around from behind the large mercenary, careful not to bump the huge beast. He held a small pistol aimed at John. He smiled, looking quite clean for someone who had been in prison the entire night.

"Traitor," John growled, his eyes glaring at the captain.

"Actually, that word describes you," the captain rebutted. "I am just a lazy, incompetent soldier, right? It was you who freed the professor. Don't you remember? I saw it with my own two eyes."

John said nothing. He scowled at his superior.

"And now you will get the wonderful chance to help us help you," Nammill said.

He stepped closer to John and whipped out the poster with a picture of the professor's creation. The paper was similar to the one John had found earlier, only newer, fresh off of the press. He tapped the picture a few times with his weapon and shook his head.

"You know what I think? I think the professor created this thing, this Galaxy Woman," Nammill said, sounding confident, reading the title of the bounty poster. "He created this powerful being just to overthrow our regime and restore his home world to the way it was. And you are going to tell me where he is."

"Not on your life!" John said, trying to sound tough, even though he was in no place to negotiate.

"For once in your pathetic, cowardly life, you're right."

Chapter 8

It was mid-morning in Ombrick. People were bustling to and fro as if they weren't sure of their purpose. Yet there was purpose underneath the chaos. They were looting the scene of last night's fire, much to Cakk and Wilson's dismay.

"Get out of here," Wilson yelled at two teenage boys who were digging in the rubble left from Dr. Nolan's house. "This stuff belongs to someone else."

"Brother," Cakk responded between a few hacks, "We look like looters, too. They don't know that the professor sent us here."

An older woman snatched some food from under a piece of wood and scampered off behind some huts. Cakk shook his head at the poverty and desperation of this town. Much of Planet York III lived like this. Humans were fending for themselves because survival was their highest priority, and small towns suffered the worst of it. Once Admiral Raynger's regime took over the planet, most of the concentration was focused on the capital city because much of the technology and weaponry was located there. It was also a key strategic location for defending against alien attackers from the mountains.

"What are we looking for again?" Wilson asked as he tossed a large rock to his left.

"I'm looking for anything I think the professor can use," Cakk answered, holding up a beaker with a black rubber seal. "Like this."

They both paused for a moment staring at the liquid inside the beaker. It was a clear liquid that seemed to refract the sun's light strangely. Every few moments it would bubble and dissipate inside the beaker. The liquid appeared to be alive. Cakk placed the container gently into this backpack. He wiped his sweaty forehead and resumed digging.

"Ahh, there they are," a male voice suddenly said.

Cakk and Wilson could not believe their eyes. The professor, grinning from ear to ear, was standing in the middle of his crumbled house, holding two golden metal plates. He bent over and dug up two more tubes from the rubble.

"Professor?" Wilson said. "What are you doing? You could get killed!"

"Bah!" Dr. Nolan scoffed. "They aren't going to look for me here. Those stupid soldiers think I'm still in the city. They wouldn't guess an old man like me could get this far alone. Besides I couldn't trust you two to find what I will need."

"How did you get here?" Cakk asked, stepping through the junk over to the professor to conceal the old man from the looters.

"I stowed away on the morning transport," Dr. Nolan said. "It's quite convenient that they don't check for tickets anymore."

"They might not be looking for you here now, but I'm sure once they determine you aren't in Lyonne, they will come here next," Wilson said angrily.

"Is that everything? What else do we need?" Cakk asked.

"We need everything!" Dr. Nolan said looking at Cakk as if he was stupid.

"Professor," said Cakk putting his hand on the old man's shoulder trying to calm him.

"Don't rush me," Dr. Nolan said, pushing Cakk's hand off. "I need everything to save my daughter."

Cakk glanced at Wilson with a disgruntled look. He didn't want to cause too much commotion for fear the locals might alert the police. He leaned toward the professor's ear as the old man continued to push away rubble.

"We can't bring everything, professor, but we'll bring what we can," Cakk said, trying to sound trustworthy.

"Then let's get to work," Dr. Nolan said, stuffing his pockets with some small glass tubes. "We haven't much time."

The alien mercenary pushed John into the middle of one of Lyonne's city streets, poking him in the middle of his back with his pistol. John stumbled but continued to walk. Vara, tugging and pulling in the opposite direction, was dragged closely behind, tears beginning to form in her eyes. This was not how she envisioned herself dying. She couldn't see the expression on John's face, but she knew that the events that were about to transpire would destroy him. The mercenary smacked John across the back of the head, sending him tumbling to his knees. Slumping on his knees, John stared at the mountain range to the northeast of the city landscape, the red sun beating on his forehead. Without turning around, John could hear the other two soldiers throw Vara to the dusty ground.

"We should do this ancient style," Nammill said, grinning as he circled John, glaring into his eyes.

"What's that supposed to mean?" John asked, not really wanting to know the answer.

"I once read about an ancient civilization that would drag their insolent people into the middle of their cities and throw stones at them until they died. How barbaric!"

Vara scowled as Nammill chuckled at the idea.

"Lucky for you, I'm all out of stones. We have better ways of punishing people now," the captain exclaimed as the signaled to the other officers. "More civilized ways."

The taller of the two officers who accompanied Nammill reached into his back pocket and pulled out five medium, silver-plated rods. The other officer pulled out a V-shaped device and handed it to the taller one. The regime called this torture mechanism the Lightning Rod. This well-known and well-feared device was four feet long and could bolt dangerous jolts of electricity into its victims. Vara could feel the heat of the device as soon as the soldier turned it on.

The soldier bolted Vara with the Lightning Rod just below her rib cage. She screamed through her chattering teeth. He quickly withdrew the weapon as Vara collapsed onto the dusty brown street. The soldier seemed surprised at the strength of the weapon, but he hovered over Vara ready to poke her again. John closed his eyes, hoping this would end soon. Vara's screams lured a few of Lyonne's inhabitants from their houses to watch and pray for her. Nammill, seeing these spectators, spoke up louder.

"This is what happens to traitors!" he yelled, pointing at John. "I will ask only one time. Where is the professor?"

"Don't tell him, John!" Vara said, trying to muster some strength. "They'll kill him!"

John's silence was enough for Nammill. He motioned for the soldier to shock Vara again.

This time the pain was unbearable. Vara shook wildly as the fire and pain penetrated her body, flowing from her toes to the back of her neck. The soldier withdrew and smoke began to rise from her body. Vara clinched her jaws so tight she could barely speak. Her eyes streamed with tears.

"John," she mumbled just enough for him to hear. "Dr. Nolan's creation might be our only chance."

John knew what Vara meant. This moment was a perfect microcosm of what history could be like forever on Planet York III. Living under a tyrant was no way to exist. There was so much more to life than survival. Soon generations of this planet would never know that. John was one of the few who did. He had a choice to make.

"Take me, Nammill," John said angrily.

"I can't kill you," Nammill said through a sinister smile. "You have to be tried and executed like all the other traitors. If I kill you, you won't have a voice. She, on the other hand, doesn't need a voice." He motioned for the guard to shock Vara again.

The pain was almost numbing this time. Vara lay on the ground shaking; her hair and skin were beginning to singe. Vara's screams echoed through the entire city. More of Lyonne's inhabitants were now watching the riveting execution of an innocent woman. Many wanted to stop this madness, yet they all felt powerless. John's voice could barely be heard through the screams. Nammill signaled for the officer to cease.

"What did you say?" Nammill asked, leaning in to hear John speak.

John couldn't tell if Vara was still alive. He wanted so badly to run and comfort her. He listened desperately, trying to hear the sound of her breathing, but there was nothing. His spirit was broken again.

"The professor is in Ombrick."

Lilac and Penn dropped their backpacks carelessly to the ground. They both were breathing heavily from the jog. Ty looked into his scanners. Hilton sat on the ground and began to unpack, looking for some type of device.

"We'll stay here until dusk," Ty said. "The path to the city is too wide open and we can't risk getting caught by the local police."

Ty slung his pack to the ground and unzipped the back compartment. He reached inside and pulled out a small, black case. He opened it up, grabbed a small pill, and tossed it into his mouth.

"We have to remember to eat," Ty reminded the other agents. "We have to keep up our strength."

"Hilton," Ty continued. "I'm going up to that tree there to get a better look at the city."

Hilton nodded, continuing to fumble with the cords and devices again. He paused and reached into another compartment of his backpack. He lifted out a small cage and gently placed it on the ground. He pushed the metal release button, and a small furry creature with four tiny legs and long whiskers scampered off into the brush.

"Hopefully, it won't be back soon," Hilton muttered.

Lilac, Penn, and Vince quickly took their energy pills and began to talk. Since Ty was out of earshot, they could be honest with each other.

"I can't believe we left Beri there with those strangers!" Vince said.

Penn, taking some medicine out of his pack, responded, "Well as long as those people are genuine, which I believe they are, she'll be fine."

"But is that the protocol?" Lilac questioned. "Do Sci-Fi agents leave their leader to die?"

"Protocol says to follow the next person in the chain of command when the original leader is unable to lead," Vince said.

"Is that what happened to Admiral Raynger?" Hilton asked, not looking up from his mess of devices.

"I completely forgot!" Vince said. "I never even looked at the data files I ripped from the patroller."

Vince rummaged into his backpack for his datapad. Lilac looked up into the trees, making sure that Ty wasn't paying attention to this little gathering.

"Here it is," Vince said, pulling out the small handheld device. "It says here that King Marquette asked Admiral Raynger for assistance in fighting off an alien invasion. Admiral Raynger responded by sending down more than half of his ship's crew to assist. He helped King Marquette win quite a few battles before returning to his ship."

"That's odd," Penn said. "You almost never hear of admirals ever leaving their ships. Usually they leave that work for lieutenant commanders."

"Listen to this," Vince said. "When Admiral Raynger returned, there was a mutiny, lead by a Lieutenant Commander Solar, whom he killed. Order was restored to the crew, but only after several hundred losses. Then King Marquette asked for assistance again."

"Realizing that he was too limited to help King Marquette and maintain command of his ship, Admiral Raynger devised a way to do both. He took a few of his most trusted agents and his best weaponry and machinery, and he came back to Planet York III to help the king. He took almost all of the supplies from the ship."

Hilton leaned in closer. "He left them up there to die," he said referring to the starving, diseased humans they encountered on the Ray Patroller.

"Raynger sealed off the bridge from within and continued to run the most basic tasks. He remotely commanded his troops on the ground. After a two-year battle, King Marquette died. There was no successor. Admiral Raynger assumed the throne."

"That makes no sense," Lilac exclaimed. "First, agents of any rank are to never assume any political offices of any governments, especially on planets that we support. Second, how can he assume the throne if he sealed himself off in the bridge?"

"I thought you said you saw his body?" Penn questioned, wondering about the mystery.

"I did," Vince explained. "It was a skeleton in an Admiral's suit. It could have been an imposter, though."

"Could he have cloned himself?" Lilac asked.

"I doubt it," Penn said. "But if he did, he would have done it on this planet. There is no cloning technology currently used in the force."

"Why would he put all of this in the logs? No one would ever come out here and find out what he did," Vince said.

"Ray Patroller log files are written by people and the ship's computer. I'm sure the computer wrote most of it and Admiral Raynger just was too lazy to destroy the records. Should we tell Ty about this?" Hilton asked.

"Tell me what?" Ty asked, suddenly appearing behind Hilton.

The agents looked from one to the other, each waiting for someone to start speaking.

Hilton started, "It appears that the government regime of this planet is run by Sci-Fi Force."

"That's ridiculous!" Ty scoffed.

"It's in the logs from the Ray Patroller," Vince replied.

"That can't be," Ty said, starting to sound nervous. "That's a violation punishable by exile. Who was the leader?"

"Admiral Raynger," Vince replied, having no other answer that would seem reasonable.

"But…" paused Ty.

"We know," agreed Penn. "He's dead."

Just then, there was the sound of engines in the distance. The agents could sense potential danger nearby. Hilton and Penn pulled out their weakly charged pistols, hoping they wouldn't need them. Ty put the scanners up to his eyes and glanced in the direction of the noise. He motioned for the other agents to take cover.

A cloud of dust was heading in their direction. As the sound came closer, Ty could see two small transport vehicles hovering above the ground. Each vehicle had two passengers, one driving and the other holding a weapon. The transports came close to the grove of trees and zipped past them, kicking up dust and small rocks. They were heading toward the agents' landing site.

"They are looking for us," Penn said.

"Are there agents aboard?" Lilac asked.

"It's hard to see," Ty said. "But if those are agents, then they are probably rogue, not to be trusted."

"Which means we are their enemy," Vince said, stating the obvious.

"I hope they don't find Beri," Hilton said.

Beri lay in a tattered, old, rusty smelling, bed. She opened one eye slowly, carefully. She glanced around the tiny bedroom. Her head throbbed. There was quite a bit of orange light shining into the room through an open window over the bed. Beri was trying to remember the events that had put her in this strange place, but most of the memories were blurry. She rolled over and immediately felt pain all throughout her body, especially her back. Now she remembered being hit by the Light Ripper.

She felt like she'd been in a war. She turned, sat up, and put her feet on the warm, wooden floor. Beri listened, waiting to hear some sound that indicated she was in friendly territory. Instead she heard nothing, at least nothing she recognized.

Suddenly there was a knock at the front door. Beri remained quiet. Then she heard voices.

"Yes, Officer?" a female voice asked.

"A spaceship landed a few meters from here. Where are the passengers? Where is the ship?" a stern male voice asked.

"I don't know what you are talking about," the farmer's wife said.

"Out of my way!" the officer commanded.

The woman screamed and there was a sound of her falling to the ground.

"I know you are hiding someone in there. And I'm going to flush them out!"

The sound of an engine grumbling quickly filled the house. Beri knew she had to get out of there quickly.

Chapter 9

Beri knew she was running out of time. The tiny room had only two exits: the small window over the bed, which she would just barely be able to get through, or the door. The door was too risky. Beri had no information about these people who were looking for her and where the other agents were. These intruders might kill her on sight. She also didn't know what this machine would do. Its humming noise was getting louder by the moment, causing her head to throb even more. She went over to the door and tried to peek through the crack between the door and its hinges. She could see gas filling the outer room.

"They are trying to smoke me out," she muttered to herself.

She glanced to her right at the small table in the corner of the room. She noticed two pills, both the same size but two different colors. One was an energy pill. The other she wasn't sure, but if her companions had left them for her she knew that she should take them. She feverishly grabbed both, shoved them in her mouth, and went over to the window. She mustered all the strength she could and began to hoist the window open. It didn't budge.

"Just great!" Beri said with frustration.

She could begin to feel some of the gas filling the room. She looked closely at the hinges of the window, trying to see if she could break the seal. Beri started to cough and her eyes started to water. She turned around and saw the green gas pouring through the cracks around the door's edges. There was no other way out.

Beri walked over and grabbed the small table. She knew it would make a lot of noise, but she'd rather risk the commotion than to die without a fight. She threw the table through the window, sending glass and broken wood flying everywhere. She could see that the hole was barely large enough for a child to get through, but she had no choice.

She reached her hands through the jagged hole and her head followed. Her skin snagged on a piece of glass and the pain was unbearable as she pulled her left shoulder through the opening. She lifted her chest over the window's ledge as she felt her upper back being stuck by tiny glass pricks. She looked up to see where she was going to fall once her waist and legs were through.

"Well, well," said a medium-built man with curly brown hair. He had a weapon aimed at her face. "Get her out of there."

Two other men, whom Beri did not initially see, pulled her through the window, raking her skin across the leftover glass. As she slammed onto the hard, dry ground, a few pieces of glass jammed into her thighs. One of the men who had pulled her through the hole pointed a long stick at her.

"Anyone else in there?" he asked.

"No," she said.

He believed her. He reached his hand to his mouth and spoke into some communicator, "We got 'em. Reporting to base in approximately fifteen minutes."

"Get her in the transport," he said, turning his back and walking toward a vehicle hovering close by.

Just as one of the men reached to grab Beri's arm, she kicked the silver stick away from her body and flipped the other man on his back. She got up from the dirt and began to run, as fast as her crippled body would let her. As she cleared the side of the house, a fourth man came from the side of the house and punched her in the stomach. Beri crumpled to the ground, gasping for air. The other officer walked up behind her and shocked her with the Lightening Rod. The pain from the electricity was unbearable and Beri passed out.

Five aliens surrounded Altaira and provoked her with their staffs. They simultaneously approached her, intending to knock her to the ground. Altaira swiftly spun around and knocked two of them down in the process. Then she jumped up, as the two others tried to hit her knees. She came down with a hard thud, hitting one of the aliens on its head. She swiftly turned to block two more attacks, and hit both aliens' arms, causing them to drop their weapons.

"Amazing," Maco said proudly. "A few hours ago, you'd never seen our fighting technique and now you've mastered it enough to fight five of our best warriors at the same time."

"I'm weak," Altaira said. A few small light spheres fell from her arms.

"Let's take you over here," Maco said, pointing to an area in the cave where red sun light shown through to the rock.

He whispered something to the other aliens and a few came over to help Altaira walk to the spot Maco suggested. The aliens who were there quickly moved out of her way and Altaira sat down weakly. Maco wrapped the purple cape around her body. Instantly Altaira began to feel better.

"Any moment now we should be ready," Maco said. "You, my gem, will lead the way."

"Why me?" Altaira asked.

"For many reasons. Do I have to explain the strategy to you again?"

"Yes, please."

"Well," Maco began, "You are by far the most powerful warrior. Most of the resistance will be directed at you and only you can fight it off. That will allow us to focus on capturing the leader and his castle. The quickest way to victory is always the best."

"What about those?" Altaira asked, pointing to three very large animals that were being herded to some other parts of the caves. "Why don't those lead us?"

"Those Mampi are very useful in battle, but they cannot fly. Only you can fly, and our enemy has flying machines that only you can stop."

"Isn't there some other way?"

"Some other way to make Mampi fly? No. They are too big."

"No," Altaira insisted. "Some other way instead of fighting."

"I thought you wanted to fight?"

"I wanted to learn the fighting style, but I don't want to fight. Can't we just share the honey?"

"No!" Maco shouted, becoming angry and impatient. "If we give them the honey they will kill us all!"

Altaira was bewildered by his response.

"They will kill you, too," Maco said sternly. "Humans are greedy. They will steal, kill, and do whatever it takes to get what they want. If you give them honey, they will want more. If you refuse, the wars will start again. Millions of years ago, all of the humans lived on the same planet. Do you know what happened? Do you know why they left?"

Altaira shook her head.

"They destroyed it, their own home planet, because they were too greedy and selfish to work together to save it. So rather than fix it, they left. I'm not going to let that happen here. They are a wasteful, pathetic species and they do not deserve my honey. They don't deserve to exist!"

Altaira had nothing to say. She felt terrible for upsetting the only being on this planet that had shown her any kindness. However, she couldn't help but wonder if Maco was being honest with her.

"I understand if you don't want to help us," Maco said, attempting to change the mood. "Altaira, you are very special. You have power that few in this universe have. I would hate to see you waste it. This war must come to an end tonight. It will either be aliens or humans left on this planet. But it cannot be both."

"What about me?"

"There's no room for those who don't pick sides."

Maco stood up and walked away, heading toward the alien army. They were hastening their pace as they prepared for the war. Altaira sat, basking in the red sunlight. She had to make a choice. She had to pick a side.

Wilson slowed the small hovercraft and parked it beside their small house. He and Cakk exited the vehicle cautiously and took in their surroundings. The street where they landed was strangely quiet for this time in the late afternoon. Cakk didn't see anyone walking around so he popped the latch to the storage compartment on the back of the hovercraft. Dr. Nolan popped up out of the compartment.

"It was hot in there," he said.

Dr. Nolan ran into the house quickly. Cakk and Wilson followed.

"Vara! John!" Wilson called out.

There was no answer. Dr. Nolan immediately went into the kitchen and poured out all of his spoils onto the table. He began to sift through the piles of metal and glass, searching for something specific. Cakk dumped his pile onto the same table and went into the bedroom to look for Vara and John.

"They're not here," Wilson said. "Why would they leave?"

"You don't suppose…" Cakk paused in the middle of his thought, not wanting to think the worst.

"I'm going to find out," Wilson said, heading out the front door.

Cakk grabbed the back of his shirt. "Wait, brother. If they were captured, they were surely forced to reveal the professor's location."

"Then they are in Ombrick," said Wilson, "looking for him."

Both the brothers peered into the tiny kitchen. The old scientist was giggling to himself while assembling a small device. He was completely unaware of the danger surrounding him. Cakk and Wilson looked at each other.

"What do you suppose we do?" Wilson asked.

Lowering his voice, Cakk said, "First, we should secure the perimeter."

Not sure what to expect, Wilson decided to take a chance and walked over to the bedroom closet. He flung the door open but no one was inside. Cakk breathed a sigh of relief.

Wilson reached up onto the top shelf and pulled out a small lock box. He put it on the bed and pounded on its top. A clicking sound followed and then the lid flipped open. Inside the box were two small, illegally purchased pistols. Wilson tossed the grey one to his brother and he inspected the red one for himself.

"Fully charged and ready for action," Wilson said.

"Let's check outside."

The two brothers split up and began combing the outside of the house. Wilson slowly and quietly opened the back door. Cakk walked past the professor towards the front door. Dr. Nolan giggled to himself as he held one of the devices up to the overhead light hanging above the small kitchen table. He appeared to be holding a golden bracelet.

"One down, one to go," the professor said to himself.

Cakk shook his head at the professor. He was amazed at how this brilliant man didn't even notice him sneaking around the house with a weapon in hand. Suddenly the front door swung open. Cakk was ready to fire, but there was now a gun pointed at his face.

The prison was freezing, dark, and solemn. John stared into the emptiness, facing one of the stone walls that was connected to his cell. A few drips of dirty water fell onto his head. He kept repeating the same words.

"I'm sorry," he said. "I'm so sorry."

Then a muffled cough came from the cell he was facing. It sounded weak, almost inaudible, but recognizable.

"I forgive you," a female voice said.

"Vara?"

She coughed again.

"Are you okay?"

"I'm with you," she responded softly.

Vara could only gaze up at the stone wall that separated them. She was too weak to sit up. Even in her dismay, Vara was somewhat optimistic. John could sense a slight smile on her face

---

“Remember, class,” Dr. Nolan said, “Do not over-mix the two gels in the bio-tubes. Come look at the examples here at my desk.”

The professor held up two shiny, clear beakers for his entire student body. In one beaker, there was a red gel that seemed to lash out at the sides. In his opposite hand, he held a green gel that was tranquil and calm like undisturbed water.

“Awesome!” John said.

“You think?” Vara questioned sarcastically.

She knew John was obsessed with science and that he and the professor were very close friends. He made the perfect lab partner, and she was secretly fond of him. It was not a secret, however, to the other students in the class, but John hadn’t noticed, yet. Vara scooted closer to John as she continued to listen to Dr. Nolan’s lecture.

“You will notice that if I put these two opposing organisms next to each other,” the professor said, continuing with his demonstration, “they are alerted to the other’s presence and they appear not to like that closeness.”

The green gel immediately began to splash onto the side of the beaker closest to the red gel, and the red gel returned the favor.

“I dare not leave them this close for long since I have no idea what would happen if these beakers break,” the professor said through a chuckle as he separated the two beakers.

Then without warning, three heavily armed men stormed into the classroom. They began pointing their weapons at the students. One of the men blocked the only exit and the other two held down the perimeter, locking their eyes on their victims.

“By order of the late King Marquette, all males must confirm their allegiance by joining the army,” bellowed the man blocking the door. “Those who refuse will be terminated immediately.”

Most of the class was terrified, but Dr. Nolan remained calm. He had heard of this new regime, a mixture of King Marquette’s old army and a new army from space pulling crazy stunts to weed out dangerous individuals. They were trying to strengthen their resistance and hold off a civil war. Since the professor had nothing to lose, he approached one of the armed men.

“Surely the army cannot use a washed up professor like me for anything.”

“Shut up, old man,” said the guard closest to the professor. “We will deal with you later.”

"This is ridiculous!" exclaimed Dr. Nolan. "Not everyone was intended to carry weapons and detonate bombs. These students will be able to serve the regime in other ways. Just give them time."

The guard at the door fired his weapon at a male student who was not even looking his way. The electrode pellet embedded itself in the young man's neck and he fell to the floor shaking and writing in pain. After a few moments, he lay deathly still.

"Oh my God!" Dr. Nolan screamed. He wanted to rush to his fallen student, but he didn't dare tempt these ruthless guards any further.

"Now," the guard warned, "if you don't want that to be you, walk outside and join the line. Those who stay will end up like that."

John glanced at Vara. Her eyes were filled with fear, yet her face seemed calm. John never felt like anything bad would happen when she was around. Even so, the weapons pointed at their heads were too hard to ignore. John was the first to slowly walk toward the door. A few of the other male students followed his lead. Just before he left the room, John looked at Vara again. She appeared calm and full of hope. Just as the last of the young male students entered the hallway, the classroom door was shut. John flinched as he heard eight shots fired, one for each of the male students who had remained in the room.

The main door to the prison corridor opened. John scooted toward the bars, attempting to see who was entering. John could barely see a patrolman carrying someone out of the gates. He looked over and saw the door to Vara's cell open. John panicked.

"No!" he shouted. "Leave her alone!"

A patrolman popped around the cell bars and pointed a Lightening Rod in John's face. "Silence, traitor!"

John quickly backed away from the stick. He slid to the back of the cell. He folded his knees to his chest and wrapped each arm around the other. John waited and listened. He heard the sound of a lifeless body being dumped onto the hard stone floor in Vara's cell. The cell bars closed with a clang. He saw three patrolmen march out of the corridor, and they locked the main door behind them. The corridor was quiet again.

"You okay, Vara?" John asked, hoping she would answer.

"Vara?" he yelled louder, fearing the worse.

"I'm alright, John," she answered softly.

"Who did they put in the cell with you? What do they look like?"

Vara, who was just as curious as John, struggled to move closer to the lifeless female body that had just been dumped onto the cold stone floor. Her face was covered by brown curly hair. She was dressed in a blue military uniform that had been torn and ripped in multiple places. She appeared to have been beaten badly. Vara scooted closer and leaned over to see if she was still breathing.

"She's alive," Vara said quietly. "She looks like a military woman."

"Military?" John asked. He scooted closer to the wall. "Does her outfit look like mine?"

"No, but it is similar."

Vara recognized the uniform from her recent past. She couldn't immediately place where she had first seen the uniform. But as soon as a wave of fear washed over her, she remembered why the uniformed triggered her memory.

"She's a member of Sci-Fi Force!" she screamed. She immediately backed away from the woman.

"Vara, that can't be." John said. "What's the name on her badge?"

"I don't see a badge."

"Does she have a communicator on her? You have to take it from her if she does."

Vara was feeling apprehensive about approaching this comatose woman. She knew John's instructions were critical, so she slowly crawled toward the other woman. Vara tried to look over the woman's motionless body without touching her. She was scanning for anything that resembled a communication device. Just then the woman backhanded Vara in the face and grabbed her arm.

"What the hell are you doing?" she asked angrily.

"I just want to know your name," said a frightened Vara, trying to loosen the woman's grip on her arm.

"Then just ask, stupid," the woman responded, releasing Vara's arm. "It's Captain Beri Onex."

"Captain?" John and Vara said simultaneously.

"Yes, Captain Beri Onex of Sci-Fi Force."

Vara backed away from Beri again, not sure of what this agent would do. John scooted closer to the wall that separated them.

"Why are you here?" John asked. "You aren't in the local militia."

"No kidding," Beri said. "I'm here on a mission that has nothing to do with you or this timid one. Any idea how I can get out of here so I can go home?"

"I was hoping you would tell us that," John said in defeat.

Once again John's hopes were dashed. They would all surely be executed in the morning. John turned to look out his tiny cell window. He noticed something strange in the distance. John squinted to get a better look through the tiny hole. Suddenly they could hear rumblings from within the mountains.

This was a sound that John hadn't heard since he was a little boy. As soon as he recognized the sound, he could hear five Naemith dragons approaching with loud screams. Vara and Beri both stood up when the sound reached them.

"Oh my God!" Vara said, covering her mouth in fear.

"They are coming!" John said, as he backed away from the cell's outer wall. "And they will kill us all."

Ty and the agents covered their ears at the deafening sound that echoed from the mountains not far from their encampment. Smoke and dust blew around them as something disturbed the wind currents.

"What the hell was that?" Hilton asked.

Ty quickly pulled out his datapad and recorded the noise while keeping one ear covered. Out of the corner of this eye he noticed that the scout rodent had returned and was patiently waiting for Hilton to reopen the trap.

"That's not a good sign," Penn said as Hilton reached down and unlocked the trap. The rodent scampered in quickly. "Normally when the scout returns, that means..."

"Bad news," Lilac finished.

"We don't have a choice now," Ty said. "Pack up your stuff. We are going to have to move."

Just as Ty barked out his orders, the agents could feel the ground start to rumble. There was a deep, resounding beat moving through the earth, almost as if the ground was a giant bass drum. Ty slung his backpack over his head and rushed over to the nearest clearing so he could take a look at what was happening. The other agents followed, except for Hilton, who was still trying to gather all of his gadgets and contraptions.

Deep from within the planet, the heavy, looming beat of massive drums sounded. Dust and rock began to move through one of the clearings that that led through the mountain range. Suddenly a blue dragon with scales flew from out of the peaks and began to move toward the city. The beast was shortly followed by four more creatures with gigantic purple wings that cast gigantic shadows on the ground as the sun's rays bounced off their blue hides. The agents stared in awe at this incredible sight. Ty turned around looking for Hilton.

"What are those things?"

Hilton quickly typed their description into his datapad. "They are Naemith dragons. They are native to the mountains of this planet."

"Dare I ask if they are fire breathing?"

"Not these ones," Hilton responded, shoving the datapad back into his pocket.

"I wouldn't put that away so soon," Penn said as he pointed toward the commotion coming from the mountains. "What are those?"

Ten large, brown, four-legged creatures that looked similar to large hippos were making their way through a mountain pass toward Lyonne. There were aliens sitting on top of each creature.

Hilton pulled his datapad back out of this pocket quickly.

"Those are Mampi being ridden by…"

Hilton paused and typed in something else in his datapad. "Hideons. They are native aliens who move around in camouflage and darkness. They have great night vision and excellent weaponry skills. The Mampi are relatively docile animals, but they are usually used in war as tanks. Their hides are almost impenetrable.

"That's our cover," Ty said. "We should be able to follow this commotion into the city. Once we get there, we can regroup."

"Maybe we can find Beri, too," Lilac chimed in with hope, referring to the two transports that had passed by their encampment heading back to the city a few moments before.

"Let's hope so," Ty said. "We better get moving."

Ty fastened his backpack tighter around his shoulders. He glanced back at the other agents who were also bracing themselves for the unknown. As he looked ahead, he could see more creatures moving from within the mountains. The dust was swirling and the wind picked up pace as the Naemiths began to flap their wings more intently. The drumbeats were getting louder. The Mampi were also picking up speed as they moved closer toward the city. Thousands of aliens armed with weapons were flowing out of caves, cracks, and chasms from the mountain ranges, and joining in the commotion heading toward Lyonne.

Ty broke from the trees into a sprint, one hand clutching a strap of his backpack and the other holding a small pistol. The other agents followed. Ty signaled for them to split up and spread out as they continued to run toward the capital city. They did as directed, placing Ty in the middle of the group, each agent with approximately one hundred yards in between them. They ran hard, blindly into this commotion, into this war, and quite possibly to their deaths.

Chapter 10

"Exactly where do you think you are going?" the gruff bounty hunter growled at Cakk.

The professor, who was in Vara's kitchen laughing, unaware of what was going on, was the center of attention for this military regime. Cakk didn't have much choice but to lay down his weapon. He did so slowly and raised both of his hands in the air to show that he was unarmed. At this point he could only hope that his brother would come from around the corner of the house.

Unfortunately, Wilson was escorted around from behind the house with two armed police officers just behind him. The setting sun showed its red rays through the city buildings as it reflected off the officer's helmets. As Cakk began to feel defeated, a resounding boom sounded throughout the city. It was immediately followed by consecutive beats that rocked the ground where they stood. The alien turned to look at the two officers who were holding Wilson. One of the officers loosened his grip on Wilson's arm and reached for his communicator. Cakk and Wilson saw their chance. It was now or never.

While the bounty hunter was still looking at the officer to see what was happening, Cakk slammed the rifle back into the alien's big snout. The large creature stumbled backward and Cakk grabbed the nozzle of the rifle. Wilson slammed his foot down on the officer who was still holding his right arm and swung a punch with his left arm that landed square on the officer's jaw. The officer wrestled with Wilson as he tried to reach for his pistol. The bounty hunter fired two shots in the air as Cakk wrestled with him to gain control of the weapon. Wilson turned and knocked the other officer's gun to the ground and kicked his communicator toward the front door.

Dr. Nolan, who no one had noticed standing at the entrance, casually picked up the communicator, and aimed Cakk's weapon at one of the officers. The old man fired, hitting the officer squarely in his right knee, causing him to crumple to the ground. He screamed from the pain.

Cakk and Wilson were stunned and they stopped fighting as the professor turned his aim toward the bounty hunter. "I suggest we stop this foolishness," Dr. Nolan said. "In a few moments this will all seem moot."

Dr. Nolan turned up the volume on the officer's communicator and they suddenly heard, "We are under attack! I repeat, we are under attack!" a mechanical voice said, amidst the booms that were resonating throughout the city.

Dr. Nolan dropped the communicator on the dusty ground and walked back into the house carrying Cakk's weapon. The officer who was still standing wrestled free of Wilson's grip and scampered away towards the castle, leaving his wounded partner. The bounty hunter, who had had a few moments to regain some strength and composure, ripped his rifle from Cakk's grip.

"This is not finished, puny human," the alien snarled.

The bounty hunter glared at Wilson and Cakk and he turned to follow the officer toward the castle. As soon as he disappeared from view, Cakk and Wilson began to focus on the impending battle that was foreshadowed by the beating drums. The two brothers glanced at each other and quickly ran into the house, heading for Vara's kitchen. They saw Dr. Nolan finishing another experiment.

"Professor!" Wilson exclaimed. "We have to get out of here and to a safe place. The police will return here looking for you whenever this commotion ends. We need to go to a place where they won't find you."

Just then a huge explosion sounded outside. Cakk glanced at his brother and they ran toward the front door to see what was happening. Dr. Nolan gathered a few trinkets and followed. He stopped just behind the two tall young men and stood on his tiptoes. Dr. Nolan couldn't believe what he saw.

Five gigantic Naemiths were circling the capital city of Lyonne. Floating in the center of the howling dragons was his creation, the glowing female. The wind currents created by the Naemiths caused her purple cape to flap broadly and her jet black hair to whip around her clear, white face. She threw small light spheres from her hands at the armored tanks that were trying to shoot her out of the sky. The tanks overturned at the impact of her attacks. A few smaller, flying interceptor pods were launched from the Lyonne castle bunkers. They were trying to create a diversion in order to get the cannons prepped for a barrage.

"She's powerful," Dr. Nolan said. "But that sneaky Maco has convinced her to join his useless crusade."

Dr. Nolan forced himself in between Cakk and Wilson and onto one of the city's main streets. Amidst the chaos of the explosions, scattering Lyonne inhabitants, overturned tanks, and pounding drums, the professor stood, staring straight up into the sky at his creation, waiving his arms.

Wilson, shocked by Dr. Nolan's last move, began to chase after him into the streets. Cakk quickly followed his brother.

"What's he doing?" Cakk asked. "He's going to get himself killed!"

Wilson responded between a few breaths, "I think he's trying to get her attention."

Just as Wilson and Cakk reached Dr. Nolan, she noticed him. An eternity seemed to pass when father and daughter locked eyes. For a moment there was an eerie familiarity from both parties, even though they had never met before. Just as Wilson began to pull the professor from the middle of the street, Lyonne's main cannon blasted his creation down from the sky. The impact caused a flash of blue and white light immediately followed by a white sphere crashing down somewhere just a few yards from the three men. The sound of the impact resonated deep within the professor's bones. Dr. Nolan suddenly gained an immense amount of strength as he turned toward Wilson and ripped his arm from the man's grip.

"I'm not losing her this time! She's all I have left."

Nammill scurried toward the city's west wall with a pack of ten soldiers directly behind him. He began barking orders.

"Make sure they don't get over that wall."

A few soldiers broke from the pack to obey his orders.

"You over there!" he said turning around. "Turn on all the militant robots. We are going to need all the fire power available."

"Yes, sir," two soldiers responded as they scampered in different directions.

There were only three soldiers behind Nammill at this point. He turned and scanned the tops of the city walls. He could see Lyonne's soldiers climbing into the cannons perched atop each of the four wall corners. He didn't see anyone protecting the south wall.

"You!" Nammill shouted at one soldier. "I need the south wall cannon repaired."

The soldier seemed shocked at this order.

"Sir? I thought Officer Vaggs took care of that."

"Vaggs," the captain said with a bit of a smirk on his lips, "has been detained."

Nammill and two remaining soldiers marched quickly toward one of the hangar bays toward the east side of the city. As the three men moved through the city, it seemed rather odd that the rest of the soldiers and militant robots were running in the opposite direction.

Nammill opened the hangar with a code that neither soldier recognized. As the steel doors slid apart, he reached around the right side of the door and pulled the lever that opened the doors that led out to the city. He spun around to the other two soldiers who stood directly behind him.

"You two must guard this hangar," Nammill said sternly. We cannot let these blasted aliens get hold of our transports."

The soldiers turned around, spaced themselves about fifteen feet apart, and stood with their weapons ready.

A few moments later there was an engine roaring behind them. The soldier on the left side of the hangar door turned around to see Nammill mounting a small hovercraft. The soldier asked, "Where are you going?"

"I have to gather the rest of the units in the surrounding cities. We don't have enough resources here," he lied.

The soldier punched in a code to close the hanger. He could barely see the captain speed away as the thick steel doors slid shut. His partner, who had barely moved since turning around, slowly turned his head to speak.

"Was he laughing?"

Hilton, Lilac, Vince, and Penn were sprinting full speed toward the city of Lyonne. The Sci-Fi Force agents were swerving between the charging aliens, the stampeding Mampi, and all of the contraptions the aliens were using to attack the city. They tried to maintain a consistent distance from each other so as to not draw too much attention to themselves. Ty, who was in the middle of the agents, lifted his communicator to his mouth.

"Take a few shots at the rogue agents," he commanded.

"Really?" Lilac questioned.

"We need to make sure these aliens don't think we are the enemy," Penn said. "They need to think we are fighting with them."

"That will buy us some more time," Ty agreed.

"But we are not supposed to attack our own," Vince exclaimed.

"Remember, these are rogue agents," Ty said. "They might start shooting at us once they pick us out of the crowd. They have more to gain by killing us first."

Ty paused his sprint, aimed his weapon, and blasted a sniper off a city wall. He didn't feel good about killing an innocent man, but he didn't have a choice now as protecting his agents was mission number one.

Hilton, who was getting tired of running, looked at a few of the smaller aliens near him. They were pushing a catapult with a launcher positioned on top. The aliens were beginning to slow down. Hilton wasn't the only one getting tired of running. He slowed down, got behind the contraption, and began to push. The machine was surprisingly not heavy at all. Noticing that he was helping him, a few of the aliens let go and began to jog along side the others chanting some war cry. Hilton smiled for a second. He glanced over at Vince, who was jogging closer. Vince joined with Hilton in pushing the weapon and the rest of the aliens decided to let these humans help with the heavy lifting.

Hilton said between a few gasps, "I figured this would remove any doubt whose side we are on."

"It will also give us some cover," Vince agreed.

Just a few yards from Penn, a cannon blasted a pack of aliens, killing them instantly. He stumbled from the impact and fell to his knees. Gathering a few breaths from the sprinting, he took this chance to take a shot at agents he saw perched on the city wall. He hit one of the agents.

Ty, who was the farthest ahead of the group, turned back quickly to see where the others were, and he reached for his communicator.

"As soon as the wall is breached, penetrate the city and meet back here at my beckon. I'll try to clear an entry on my way in and then duck out of the main fighting. Hopefully there will be some dwellings that can provide temporary cover."

"Roger," the agents replied one after another between breaths.

Ty dodged a few gunshots from automatic guns stationed against the city walls. He noticed a Mampi coming next to him. As he neared the wall with this huge animal charging behind him, the gunfire began to increase. He made his running path more sporadic. Looking at the thick city wall just ahead, Ty began to wonder, "How are we going to get through there?"

John gazed out in horror at what was transpiring just outside the prison cell. The location of the prison provided a great view to see all of the action. Perched high in one of the prison's five towers, John could see one of the Naemiths continue its circular path of intimidation.

"What's happening?" Vara asked.

"Sounds like a war," Beri said. She found it annoying to be around such a useless female.

Vara could feel Beri's disdain and she ignored her terse response. She asked again, "Is it the aliens?"

"Yes," John answered, turning to face the two women. "It looks like they've emptied their caves."

The three prisoners paused as cannons fired in the distance. A few screams could be heard from injured and dying soldiers. A bright light from cannon fire shattered a housing complex and temporarily blinded him. As he struggled to regain his sight, he saw the glowing female. She was darting through the sky, firing radiating spheres from her hands and dodging cannon fire. Her flight pattern was like a humming bird, quick, slight, but purposeful. At one point she flew close to the prison tower, just a few yards from Jonathan's gaze. He thought about trying to get her attention, trying to tell her that she was fighting on the wrong side of the war.

"Any ideas of how we can get out of here?" Beri asked. "This war will be a good cover to escape."

There was no response from John or Vara. Beri rolled her eyes. These civilians were useless to her. Even though John appeared to be an officer, he didn't act like one in Beri's eyes. She stood up, stumbled a little, and nudged Vara to move out of her way. Vara gave her a warning look, but she slid to her right a few inches. Beri reached her hand through the cell bars and began to try to feel the metal lock. She probed the device with her fingers, hoping to discern some flaw. Another blast caused her to flinch and she had to start again.

"Even if you break the lock the alarm will instantly sound," John said hopelessly.

"I get that," Beri responded stubbornly. "But who's coming to respond to it?" She continued to try to pick the lock. "The entire alien army is attacking the city," Beri exclaimed. "If this castle is still standing in the morning, it's going to take the entire city state's army to respond to this madness."

"She's right, John," Vara said. "If we can break the lock, we can use the war as a diversion and flee this place."

John looked at Vara, his spirit still broken. "It still doesn't matter. If the aliens win the war they will eliminate all human life from this planet. They will start with the capital city and then proceed to the outlying communities. And if the humans win, they will hunt us down, bring us back here, and kill us. There is no way out."

Beri glanced down at the floor, picked up a small pebble and threw it directly at John.

"Ow!" John said as the small rock hit him squarely in the forehead. "What was that for?"

"You are a pathetic excuse for a soldier!" Beri screamed, her anger palpable. "You should be ashamed to wear that Sci-Fi Force uniform! I don't care if you're a rogue agent or if you've just gone crazy, but if I get out of this cell I'm going to remind you what it means to be a real Sci-Fi Force agent."

"You are going to help me get out of here," she screamed over the cannon fire outside. "Your destiny on this planet might not be of concern to me, but I have more options than just death. I'd rather take my chances out there than do nothing here in this cell."

A huge boulder suddenly came crashing into the prison wall, cracking the foundation and knocking the three unsuspecting prisoners onto the cold floor. The cell bars began to crack and bend under the weight of the breaking foundation.

Beri saw an opportunity. There was now a large break between the wall and the farthest bar in the cell. The captain stood up on her toes and pressed her back against the wall and her chest against the metal. Her hand and shoulder passed through easily but the rest of her body was now stuck. She motioned for Vara to help her.

"Push me through!"

Vara took a wide, deep stance and began to push on Beri's hips to get her through the opening. Beri winced in pain. Her body didn't move, but the walls did. The cracks in the stone ceiling were getting wider, exposing some of the dusk sky.

John shouted over the growing commotion outside the prison walls. "This place is going to collapse! You need to get out of there!"

Beri ignored John's screams and continued to push herself through the gap. Vara kept pushing, but it was to no avail. Beri looked at John's side of the prison corridor and saw that the ceiling in his cell was beginning to collapse. As the foundation of the prison continued to crumble, Beri could feel the wall beginning to push her back into the metal bar. The opening she had hoped would be big enough to squeeze through was now getting smaller. She was being crushed.

"You need to get out of there!" exclaimed John, dodging a few pieces of falling rock from the ceiling of this cell. He pulled on the bars of his cell, hoping to shake them free. Beri's face was starting to get red and she began to bleed from an open wound in her left side. The pressure was becoming too great.

"I'm stuck!"

"There she is," Cakk said, pointing to Altaira as she darted through the dimming sky.

Altaira flew in sporadic motions, shooting glowing spheres from her hands that exploded on impact. Cakk, Wilson, and Dr. Nolan had just reached the location where Altaira had crashed after being shot down by the city's main cannon. Dr. Nolan gazed in awe at the crater left from her plummet.

She had fallen badly and it showed now in her movements. They were not as sharp or as fast. The crater from her fall leveled two houses and destroyed half of another, leaving a seven-foot hole in the ground. Amidst the commotion and loud noise, Dr. Nolan noticed that the crater had small lights bouncing around in the center. He thought about climbing in to investigate, but the balls of light faded quickly. Concerned, he looked back into the sky.

Altaira was circling the city of Lyonne just beneath the Naemiths, blowing the enemy's ground tanks to pieces. Some of the hovercrafts tried unsuccessfully to knock her from the air. More soldiers were aiming their cannons and weapons in her direction. The military regime of Lyonne definitely saw Altaira as a threat. A slight smile crept onto Dr. Nolan's face as he watched her prowess, only to be wiped away a few seconds later.

Another direct hit from a cannon knocked Altaira from the sky, and this time her plummet looked even more painful. Wilson and Cakk braced the professor as she came crashing down just a few blocks from where they stood. The impact catapulted a few soldiers on the ground into the air. The sky now seemed darker without her glow above the city.

The men immediately broke into a heated sprint toward Altaira's landing spot, hoping to get there before any soldiers discovered her.

"Score!" Hilton shouted as he watched a boulder crash into one of the castle towers. Hilton gave a high five to the two aliens beside him who were chattering and celebrating in their native language. Another light sphere crashed in the distance. He picked up his communicator. "Did you see that, Penn?"

"Yes," Penn said as he rolled a boulder toward the Mampi. "But I'm pretty sure your last shot did not cause that explosion."

Hilton began to help Penn and the aliens load another boulder onto one of the Mampi's tails, which served as a giant slingshot. Just as they finished lifting the rock, one of the rogue agents on a hovering disk swooped by and shot one of the aliens. Hilton hid behind one of the Mampi's thick hind legs. Penn pulled out his pistol and shot at the retreating agent. One of his shots clipped the back of the hover disk, sending the agent flying into the ground.

"Nice shot," Ty said over the communicator. "Aim your next shot over here. We just set up a small explosive in the middle of this wall." Ty, Lilac, and Vince were just outside the city wall fighting off weapon fire from the mechanical soldiers with the aliens.

Penn lifted his night scanner to his eyes. He saw two small, flashing lights attached to the city wall. They were barely visible underneath the night sky. "Do you see it, Hilton?"

"I see it," Hilton said referring to the blinking red lights.

"Let's do this. I'll give you some cover," Penn said, getting his pistol ready.

For a moment, Hilton and Penn took in the massive battlefield between them and the great city of Lyonne. Thousands of aliens lay dead under the darkening sky. Millions more were continuing the fight against the advancing militia. Most of the Mampi were providing cover for the aliens, who were using their staffs to dislodge agents from their hovering disks. Others were rushing toward the city, throwing their staffs at agents perched on the wall. The aliens were losing despite their immense numbers.

Hilton and a few aliens steadied the Mampi for the next launch. Then the huge beast launched a boulder directly toward the wall's tiny blinking lights. Just as the boulder entered flight, a different blast exploded a few feet from Penn, knocking him to the ground. He could faintly hear Hilton screaming something from behind the Mampi. Just as his eyes started to close, Penn saw the explosion in the middle of the city wall lighting up the night sky.

Chapter 11

Another explosion rocked the castle, causing its outer walls to break and collapse. John could now feel cool air from the dark, night sky. The floor of his cell began to crack and cave from underneath his feet. John grabbed the cell bars, hoping they would support his weight and allow him time to think. He couldn't allow his mind to think about the demise that awaited him fifteen floors below.

Beri and Vara were still trying to push Beri through the quickly collapsing walls. The wall behind Beri was folding over and pushing her deeper into the metal cell bars. The entire tower was sure to collapse at any moment.

Just a few yards away and fifteen floors below from the crumbling prison, Dr. Nolan, Cakk, and Wilson were approaching the huge crater where Altaira had just landed. She tried to get up, but she collapsed back into the hole. Dr. Nolan slid down into the crater to help her up. Wilson followed behind him and ordered Cakk to stand watch for any soldiers.

Dr. Nolan reached out to Altaira and grabbed her arm softly to help her to sit up. She tried desperately to focus her tired eyes on him. She wasn't sure what to think about this strange man trying to help her. She had spent the previous few hours destroying his home, yet he showed some compassion for her. There was also a strange connection she felt to him that she couldn't place. A huge smile erupted on Dr. Nolan's face.

"You are beautiful," he said, "Just like your mother."

"Mother?"

"Yes, Sasha, just like your mother."

"My name is Altaira. Who is this Sasha you speak of?"

Wilson leaned toward Dr. Nolan. "She's got some spunk."

"I named you Sasha," Dr. Nolan explained. He paused and slowly smiled, "but if you like Altaira, then Altaira it is."

Altaira began to relax. "How do I know you?"

"Well, you see..." Dr. Nolan began.

Before he could finish, Cakk motioned from outside the pit. "We have visitors."

Maco and his alien troops suddenly surrounded the pit. Cakk and Wilson raised their hands to demonstrate that they were unarmed.

"Maco!" Altaira shouted, trying to stand up. She was still too weak to stand and she quickly fell back to the ground.

"Altaira, we are almost completely through the city walls. We must begin our last offensive on the castle," Maco commanded. He turned to point to the castle in the center of Lyonne.

"She's too weak," Dr. Nolan exclaimed, moving to protect Altaira from Maco. "She won't last much longer. Her energy will dissipate and then she will be no more."

"Who is this?" Maco spit out angrily. "Why am I listening to this weak and insignificant human?"

Without warning Maco grabbed a bow staff and threw it at Dr. Nolan's head, knocking him unconscious to the ground.

Altaira was shocked. She wasn't sure why her feelings suddenly shifted, but seeing Maco attack an innocent, unarmed man just didn't seem right. She looked at Maco, confused.

"He will meet his end soon enough," Maco declared. "Come, Altaira. Let's finish this job!"

She didn't move. No agreement, no confirmation, no denial, no argument. The night wind blew her short jet black hair around her face. The commotion of the war scattered throughout all parts of the city, but this spot seemed deathly quiet. Altaira just stared at Maco.

Maco, not wanting to show any sign of concern to the other aliens, quickly responded, "Whenever you are ready, Altaira, you can rejoin us." With that, Maco and the other aliens retreated back into the war-ridden streets of Lyonne. Their short bodies quickly disappeared into the commotion.

Cakk and Wilson stood beside Altaira as she bent over the fallen professor, lightly stroking his receding gray hair. Wilson noticed two golden bracelets lying just underneath the professor. He gently reached his hand behind the old man's back and inspected the jewelry. He handed them to Altaira.

"I think he wanted you to have these."

Altaira slowly looked up at Wilson. She reluctantly took the bracelets and put one on each wrist. "I'm sorry," she whispered into Dr. Nolan's ear. "You didn't deserve this."

Cakk, who wasn't one for solemn moments, jumped down into the crater and began lifting the professor's limp body out of the hole.

"Where are you taking him?" Altaira asked with alarm.

"He's still got life left in him," Cakk said, reassuring her. "But he won't survive out here with all this war debris flying about. He needs some shelter to recover."

As Wilson helped Cakk carry Dr. Nolan out of the hole, Altaira suddenly grabbed Wilson's shoulder. "What can I do to pay for my mistake? He did not deserve that."

For a moment, Wilson felt like a lucky guy who had just rubbed a magic lamp and was granted three wishes. He had seen a glimpse of what Altaira could do, but he didn't know the extent of her power. He could tell she was somewhat naïve, but she wasn't ignorant, either. He paused as he thought of what to say. Amidst all of this chaos, death, and destruction, he knew a few choice words could change the fate of everyone on this planet. Before he could answer, a familiar voice interrupted his thoughts.

"That's Vara!"

Wilson spun around beside Altaira, looking for the sound. It was difficult to see in the dark night sky. He heard the scream again.

"Vara!" Wilson said louder, finally focusing on where the sound was coming from.

Fifteen floors above the city streets, he could barely see three humans hanging on for dear life to a crumbling tower. He was frozen with fear as he saw the tower give way and John, Vara, and Beri tumble from the rubble. Wilson grabbed Altaira and screamed, "You have to save them!"

Altaira saw the three humans plummeting from the sky. She reached down inside herself, finding one last burst of energy, and blasted from the depths of the crater to rescue them.

Hilton was running, out of breath as he dodged a few stray bullets. He leapt behind a growing wall of dead Mampi and joined the other agents.

"Where have you been?" Ty demanded in between shooting a few rounds from his gun. "Lilac's hurt!"

"I'm alright," she insisted through clinched teeth as she wrenched in pain. There was blood dripping between her fingers as she tried to cover her wound. Vince looked around for Penn, hoping he could help Lilac.

Ty spoke up, noticing the same void, "Where's Penn?"

"He…he didn't make it," Hilton said without raising his eyes from his datapad.

Silence penetrated the group. Vince sat down on the hard, dusty ground and gazed into the night sky. Lilac and Ty paused their returning gunfire to let the disappointment set in.

"Penn got caught in a blast radius trying to cover me," Hilton continued. "I tried to grab as much of his equipment as I could."

This battle was much more than these agents bargained for. Ty assumed this mission would be a simple check and restore communications mission between two Sci-Fi factions. Instead, they were deep in a war in which they had no stake. One agent was dead, another missing, another wounded badly, and they still had no way to leave this planet or communicate with their home ship.

As the aliens continued to stream past their barricade behind the dead Mampi, Ty couldn't help feeling like a failure. Even though he had trained for circumstances like this, he discovered that reality brought out his real character. Ty scanned the faces of the three remaining agents. Lilac fired fewer return rounds amidst tears. Vince sat bewildered on the ground. Hilton continued staring at his datapad, a single tear rolling down his cheek. Ty wasn't sure he was the best leader for this group, but right now he was all they had. They could use a little hope right now.

"She's alive!" Hilton suddenly shouted. He turned to show his datapad to the group. There was a small red dot moving quickly from east to west on his screen.

"Is that Captain Onex?" Lilac asked, a little grin appearing on her face through the tears. "Have you been tracing her this whole time?"

"I wish I had," Hilton said. "Penn must have placed a device on her before we left that house."

"Well let's not waste anymore time," Ty said, not wanting to lose another agent. "Hilton, lead the way."

"Let's get to it," Hilton replied. "She's moving very fast but I think we can get her."

Ty turned around to instruct the agents. "Vince, you provide cover for Hilton, and Lilac, stay as close to Hilton as you can and try to find some cover in the city. I'll follow close behind Lilac. I think the gap in the wall should be enough to get through," Ty said, referring to the blast Penn and Hilton has created earlier.

"Orders received, Ty," Hilton said. "As soon as I get into the city, I'll try to move carefully to avoid enemy agents. I'll turn my datapad into a beacon so you can all track me."

The agents were exhausted, but they took their commands and hoped that this would be the last offensive of the night. They counted to three and began sprinting toward their target.

Ty and Vince fired their weapons at as many of the snipers as they could see. Hilton jumped into the flood of aliens during the break in gunfire. Lilac took a deep breath, gripped her throbbing shoulder, and followed after Hilton into the stampeding aliens. As Ty and Vince continued firing at the snipers, Ty wasn't so sure they would make it back to the others. They had brought too much attention to themselves, and now more gunfire was concentrated at their position. Ty had to act fast, before Hilton and Lilac were out of sight.

"Change of plans," he shouted to Vince over the gunfire. "You go out next, and I'll cover you."

Vince was initially thrown by the sudden change in the commands. He was too exhausted to question the change but he thought it odd. He glanced at Ty for reassurance. Ty nodded and Vince turned away from Ty. He jumped out from behind the fallen Mampi and scampered into the crowd of aliens running into the city. Vince could only hear Ty shouting and the gunfire increasing behind him. As Vince passed between the gaps in the city wall, one of the city cannons silenced the commotion behind him with three jolts of thunder.

Altaira flew as fast as she could through the night sky. She flew in zigzags to avoid cannon blasts and gunfire from the soldiers of Lyonne. Her sights were focused on one thing—the three falling humans just a few yards in front of her. John, Vara, and Beri were tumbling perilously with the failing rubble, hoping that someone would rescue them before they reached an excruciating end.

Just before impact, Altaira flew near and grabbed Vara's outstretched arm and John's flailing ankle. John instinctively grabbed one of Beri's wrists. Altaira swooped around, dodging the falling rock, and flew them safely back toward Wilson.

Altaira was struggling with the weight of her passengers, and it showed in her gliding height. Beri, bracing for an untimely descent, took the matter into her own hands. As they got closer to the ground, Beri wrestled her wrist free of John's grip and landed with a thud on the dusty city street. John, agreeing with Beri's move, followed. He hit the ground just as hard. He shook off the immediate pain and turned to see Altaira crash into Wilson's outstretched arms, sending the three of them tumbling into a dusty pile.

John breathed a sigh of relief. He ran over to attend to Vara. When he reached the group, he turned her body toward him.

"Thanks," she said softly.

Wilson crawled over toward his sister. "She's alright," he confirmed.

Beri sat up in the dirt and spit some blood onto the ground. She wiped her busted lip with her hand. A little dazed from the fall, she scanned her surroundings. She wasn't sure what to do next. Fortunately she wouldn't have to decide.

"Over here!" Cakk shouted from behind the door of an old, abandoned house.

Wilson grabbed Vara from John, and he motioned for the rest of the group to follow him. "Come on," he commanded.

Beri, still not sure she wanted to stay with this uncoordinated group, sat in the dirt for a few moments. She was looking warily at Altaira who was still struggling to get up. This being clearly was not human or alien. Sci-Fi Force protected many different species, but she had never seen anything like this. There was something frightening about a being with this much power that could seemingly destroy an entire civilization. Beri was tempted to let Altaira lie there and die.

As Beri watched Wilson and John disappear behind the door into the dilapidated house, Altaira crumpled back to the ground. She was staring straight into Beri's eyes. Her life and her glow were quickly fading. Beri couldn't let this creature die like this. Against her better judgment, she pulled Altaira up from the ground. "Let's go," she said.

Even though Altaira didn't weigh much, Beri's exhaustion made carrying her difficult. Altaira's head hung toward the ground and her body slumped in Beri's grasp. Halfway to the house, Beri's right knee buckled and they both collapsed to the ground. There was no one around to help them. Beri couldn't make it to the house with Altaira and she didn't want to leave the creature alone. If they stayed here too much longer, the soldiers of Lyonne or the raiding aliens would certainly decide their fate.

"Raynger!" Maco shouted as he pounded on the throne room doors. The aliens had killed most of the castle's guards on their way to the top of the palace. Now they were so close to victory, so close to the throne of Lyonne and total control of Planet York III. Maco could taste victory on his brown lips.

"Raynger!" he shouted again.

He then turned and commanded his soldiers in his native tongue. One of the aliens took his order and placed a small bomb just outside the throne room doors.

He pushed a button on top of the bomb and began to speak loudly in his native tongue. The other aliens understood and they all scattered as far as possible. Maco stood away from the ensuing blast.

The entire palace shook as the bomb exploded, sending pieces of the throne room doors in every direction. Many of the aliens covered their heads to avoid being pelted by rock and steel. Maco moved slowly forward into the smoke and dust, followed closely by his army. There was no returning gunfire from within the throne room. There were no footsteps running to protect the king of Lyonne. There was no sound at all, save the last falling pieces of the throne room doors.

The smoke cleared to reveal an empty throne room, and even more surprisingly, an empty throne. Maco and his close followers moved slowly toward the large golden chair situated atop five golden steps in the center of the room. As they entered the room, they formed a perimeter.

It seemed like a trap. But if it was a trap, the humans must have known that they were coming. Maco was cautious as he approached the throne. He took each step one at a time toward the great chair he had so long coveted. Each step moved him closer toward total victory and conquering the capital city of Lyonne. When Maco reached the top, he sat slowly and triumphantly into the throne. He placed his hands on the arms of the golden chair.

"Victory is ours!"

The aliens raised their weapons and chanted together in glorious triumph. Maco grinned broadly, showing his pointy yellow teeth. He basked in this moment as more aliens began to fill the throne room. While he wondered where Admiral Raynger had run to hide, in this moment it was of no importance. Now was the time to commence the second part of this plan.

"My friends," he shouted to the celebrating aliens, "The war is over, but there is more work to do. We must begin extermination. Any species on this planet that is not one of us must be destroyed!"

The aliens let out an even louder cheer. It was clear that they, too, had waited for this moment.

"I only ask one thing," said Maco, lowering his tone. "Bring Admiral Raynger and Altaira to me alive!"

There were eerie similarities in this situation. Two females, both in a foreign world, weak and beaten, left to die in unfamiliar streets. One was unusually far from home. The other was without a home. Both had strong hearts, but their bodies were failing them. They lay in the dirt of this city's streets, surrounded by a never-ceasing battle. Hope seemed far away, but that was not reality.

"There she is!" Hilton exclaimed as he broke into a sprint toward Beri's fallen body. Lilac and Vince were close behind him.

When they were close to Beri, their gaze was not directed at their leader, but at the creature that lay beside her.

"Was that the thing I saw flying around the city?" Hilton asked.

"Probably," Beri answered weakly.

Beri glanced at Altaira who lay face down beside her. Her glow was fading, but the light she radiated was still strong enough to alert enemies to their presence. Quickly returning to her leadership, Beri beckoned for Vince to help her up off of the dirty street. Vince gave Beri his arm and she stood up carefully and began hobbling.

"Quick," she commanded, "Get us in there."

Beri pointed toward a broken house where John and Vara had disappeared a few moments prior. Vince helped Beri hobble into the house. Hilton picked up Altaira, whose body was very limp. Lilac tried to help Hilton, but he shrugged her away.

"Your shoulder can't take much more," Hilton said, concerned. "Go ahead. I'm right behind you."

Lilac didn't argue and scampered into the house. Hilton was surprised at how light Altaira was, but his fatigue still made it difficult to carry her. He trudged through the darkness. As he reached the old house door, he turned around and slammed his back into the door, bursting through. Cakk, not sure what was happening, turned to swing a club at the intruder.

"Wait!" Beri shouted, holding up her hand.

Cakk held his swing and placed the club at his side.

"Not such a good idea to come bursting in here like that," Cakk said to Hilton.

"Well you could at least hold the door open," Hilton said, still holding Altaira. "Any place where she can rest?"

Wilson emerged from a back room. "In here," he motioned.

Hilton followed Wilson, and Beri and Cakk came behind him. Dr. Nolan lay unconscious on a mat in one corner of the room. Sitting on the dirt floor next to the professor was Lilac, who was having her shoulder bandaged by Vara. Hilton laid Altaira on the floor gently next to Lilac. He covered her with a tattered grey cloth. Beri began scanning her remaining troops.

"Where are the others?" she questioned Hilton as he stood up. Hilton couldn't find the words to tell her that Penn and Ty were gone. But Beri could see the loss in his eyes.

"How?" Beri asked softly.

Vince walked toward Beri with a bandage in his hand. He began to wrap the bleeding wound on her hip. Hilton was not going to answer the question.

"Vince?" Beri asked, hoping he would explain what happened.

"During the battle," he answered in as few words as possible. "They died bravely."

"Ty too?"

Vince shook his head again.

Beri had no words to comfort the three agents left in her crew. For a mission that was intended to be a routine reconnaissance mission, this outcome was far from foreseen. Here they were, hundreds of thousands of kilometers from home with no way in sight of getting off of this planet. Of the four agents left, only two were relatively healthy. If she was going to succeed at this mission, she needed some answers from the others in this room. She decided to start with the only person in the room wearing a Sci-Fi Force uniform, whom she did not believe deserved to wear it.

"John," she said walking toward him, "What's going on here?"

Cakk readied his club just in case the situation turned violent. Wilson steadied his brother. John, however, didn't feel quite as comfortable.

"Well?" Beri asked, becoming exasperated. "Why are you impersonating a Sci-Fi Force agent?"

"I don't know what you are talking about," he replied.

"Where did you get that uniform?" Beri was now standing directly in his face. She pulled at the shoulder cloth of his uniform to make her point. Hilton reached out and grabbed Beri's hand. Beri was shocked that Hilton was trying to hold her back.

"Their world was invaded by us," Hilton said, ashamed to admit that Sci-Fi Force was actually at fault for some of this mess in which they found themselves.

Beri stood back, astonished. "What?"

"Admiral Raynger invaded this planet and took it over years ago. He gave out Sci-Fi Force uniforms to anyone who joined his crew. That's why his uniform has the old design," Hilton explained.

"So are you with Admiral Raynger?" Beri said, turning back to John.

"No."

"I couldn't tell," Cakk muttered.

Frustrated and realizing she was getting nowhere fast, Beri changed tactics, but before she could ask another question, Vara spoke up. "How do we know you are not working for Admiral Raynger?" she asked.

Realizing Vara's point, Wilson and Cakk changed their stance toward the agents in the room. Their senses were now alerted to any abnormal moves from these intruders to their home planet.

Beri understood some of the confusion. To these natives, Sci-Fi Force was a treacherous organization of people who invaded their world and ruled it with an iron fist. She had to convince them that their reality was not the truth.

"We are not part of Admiral Raynger's faction. We came here from the RY sector to find out what happened to Admiral Raynger's crew. We noticed the light display in the outer atmosphere and feared that Admiral Raynger was under attack," Beri said, hoping to calm the tense air in the tiny room.

"Light display?" Vara said, turning to look at Altaira.

At that moment, all the dots were connected. These agents came to their planet looking for the very thing that had created Altaira. Somehow they had been dragged into this civil war and now they were searching for answers and a way home.

John responded, "You just want to get home?" Beri and her crewmembers nodded.

"If Maco has control of the palace and the throne, that will be impossible. He will shut down any interplanetary movement," Wilson explained.

"Who is Maco?" Lilac asked.

"He is the leader of the alien army," Altaira said.

The rest of the group was surprised to see her sitting up and looking more energized. The silence was awkward. Everyone in the room stared at Altaira, waiting for her to say something else.

"I helped him," she said with a guilty tone in her voice. "He said that humans were the enemy. He said..."

"It doesn't matter what he said," Vara interrupted. "He's a liar and he used you for his benefit."

"That's no excuse," Altaira responded. "I killed innocent people."

"Innocence is sometimes a point of view," Hilton said.

"But you can make it right," Beri said, sensing a moment to change her circumstances. She turned to Wilson. "You said that if we defeat this Maco, we could get off of this planet?"

Wilson nodded.

"And our home will return to normal," Vara chimed, "At least as normal as it can be, after all of this."

John stood up from the floor confidently. Altaira stood up looking more powerful than any of them had ever seen her. Her glow was much brighter and bluer. Wilson and Cakk moved closer to the standing group.

"What's your plan?" John asked.

Chapter 12

As the morning sun broke across the mountain range north of Lyonne, Maco's army of aliens began to round up all the humans they could find. They met little resistance from the common folk, many of whom were too afraid to fight back for fear of their immediate demise. There were a few skirmishes between Lyonne's remaining soldiers and small packs of aliens. The morning light would help the soldiers fight better, but at this point in the war, the probability of the tide turning was slim. Most of the city cannons were destroyed or decommissioned. Many of the still-functioning tanks were in the hands of the aliens. Maco was now controlling the militant robots, and all of the surviving mercenaries had fled. Maco would deal with those traitors later. His focus was on the humans.

Maco had already dispersed many of the aliens to the smaller surrounding cities and towns of Planet York III to ensure that any early resistance would be squashed quickly. Some of his closest companions were staking claim to territories that they could rule once the extermination was complete. Maco sat comfortably on his throne, yet he didn't feel completely secure. Admiral Raynger and Altaira were nowhere to be found.

Four aliens were leading a group of humans into the castle prisons. The aliens prodded the humans with staffs, making sure the line moved smoothly. This group of humans was a mixture of men, women, and children, but two among this group had joined for a different reason.

John and Vince stayed near the back of the caravan of the humans who were to be executed. They were both paying keen attention to their path toward the castle. John knew where the aliens were taking them, as this path mimicked his first assignment as a member of the now overthrown Lyonne army. They were walking toward the castle's underground gas chambers. Trying not to be obvious, John squinted his eyes, hoping to detect any motion near the city's southern corner of the wall. The wall was still intact, but the cannon perched atop it was apparently not functioning.

Wilson pushed Cakk up into the cannon spiral bay, trying not to grunt too loudly. Cakk quickly turned around and lifted his brother beside him with a double-hand grasp. Wilson squeezed behind his brother to the back of the bay while Cakk moved to the front.

"I hope John was right about this thing," Cakk said, popping open one of the electrical panels in the cannon.

The wires were frayed as if someone had been trying to fix the weapon. Four wires with four different colors were intertwined within the small rectangular panel. Cakk was frustrated, and he breathed a heavy sigh.

"You have time, brother," Wilson said, "But not forever."

Wilson peered out of the targeting scope and focused on the group of prisoners, particularly John and Vince. He could see the group turning down a ramp into a lower entrance of the castle.

"I hope they make it," Wilson sighed.

"What about Vara?" Cakk questioned while still trying to figure out which wires needed repair.

"She's in a part of the city that is sparsely populated. By the time the aliens find her, the plan will already be in motion. They will be too distracted to worry about two women and an old man."

"What about the other two?"

"We can only hope," Wilson said.

Beri and Hilton zigzagged through the tattered houses of Lyonne. Once they were about one hundred yards from the gap that Ty and the others had created in the city wall during the night barrage, they split up. Beri entered a row house beside the gap. Hilton scampered across the street to the opposite side and crouched down behind a crate. He took out his communicator to relay his position to Beri.

"I'm in position and ready."

"Roger," Beri said. She waited for the next response.

"Umm…not Roger," Wilson responded. "The cannon is still not working."

Beri's eyes widened. This was an unexpected turn of events.

"We have to go now," she replied. "John and Vince are almost inside the castle. Once they get inside, we will lose eyes on them."

"We'll get this piece of junk going," Wilson said, trying to sound confident.

"What now?" Hilton questioned.

"Just stand by, Hilton."

Right then a beam of light shot up from the roof of a house followed by a streaking Altaira. She zoomed high above the city and hovered. The offensive was starting now whether they were ready or not.

"Maco!" Altaira shouted, her voice booming.

Maco almost fell off of this throne. He scampered to one of the throne room windows and flung it open. There she was, his prize possession, circling the castle. His grin was quickly replaced by a frown. She didn't sound happy to see him.

"I'm here, Altaira," Maco cautiously shouted from the window. "Look at what we have done. We won. Come celebrate with me."

The pack of aliens leading the prisoners into the castle gas chambers stopped to see the commotion. John looked at Vince, making sure he would react at the right time. Altaira continued circling the castle.

"You tricked me, Maco," she shouted, pointing a finger at him. "You used me to gain your own power."

"Altaira," Maco said calmly, "You misunderstood me. This was all for you. I've been waiting here for you to take the throne."

Altaira stopped circling in an instant. She shot a questioning glance at Maco trying to figure out his true intentions. Without warning, she suddenly darted through the window into the throne room.

Beri grabbed her communicator, "What's she doing? That's not part of the plan!"

"I have no idea, but its now or never," Hilton responded. He took off running toward the dead Mampi just outside the city wall gap. He placed a blast charge into the decaying carcasses of the beasts and darted back into the city.

The aliens, who had paused to watch Altaira, resumed marching the prisoners toward the gas chambers. As the steel doors opened, John looked at Vince with widening eyes. This was not going as planned. Once they made it inside the gas chambers, there would be no way out.

Altaira halted her flight just as quickly as she had darted into the throne room. Maco dodged her entrance and turned to see her standing on the white marble floor. Altaira stood there not looking at Maco, but instead looking at the throne. She was awed by the splendor of the golden chair that sat in front of her. Maco could see her expression as he inched closer.

"Go ahead," he motioned. "Take your rightful place."

Altaira turned to look at Maco. She didn't trust him, but in this confusing world she wasn't sure whom she could trust. Had the other humans been lying to her? Was Maco really trying to help her achieve greatness, or was he a liar and traitor using her to gain his own power?

Altaira walked slowly toward the chair, not taking an eye off of Maco. She gracefully turned, whipping her purple cape around her glowing body, and sat down. From this position she towered over Maco even more than usual. Altaira wasn't sure how she felt about this, but she was even more confused about how Maco really felt.

A few of the other aliens in the room chattered amongst themselves in their native tongue.

"What are they saying?" she asked.

Maco paused before answering. "They are congratulating their new queen," he lied.

Suddenly an explosion sounded from outside. Maco rushed to the window to see what was happening. Altaira had momentarily forgotten about the plan she had devised with the others.

"There are insurgents in our midst, Altaira," Maco said. "You must destroy them!"

"Why don't you?" Altaira shot back with an air of confidence. "They pose no threat to me."

"You cannot let even a few of them grow strong, Altaira! A few can cause disruption beyond what many can imagine."

"If I am the queen," Altaira said, enjoying her new power even more, "then I command you to stop them."

Maco now sensed that the tide had turned against him. As he could hear the commotion in the city streets becoming louder and louder, he now had to focus on the only thing that could stop him. That thing sat in the throne of Lyonne.

John and Vince turned and grabbed the staffs from the two unsuspecting aliens at the rear of the human caravan. They smacked them across the head and set their sights on the two aliens at the front. Noticing the panic, the remaining humans in the line broke formation and scattered. This only helped John and Vince approach the two leading aliens.

John swung his staff, only to be knocked down to his knees. He buckled to the ground. Vince dodged and poked the other alien and knocked it back into its partner. John, noticing the distraction, knocked both aliens across the head and sent them crumpling to the ground.

"This way," he said to Vince. The two scampered around to the west side of the castle. They approached a steel door that was unguarded by the aliens. Vince thought this was odd.

"No aliens here?" he asked.

"They don't know the code."

John expertly punched four buttons on a red-lit panel just to the right of the door. The steel door slowly lifted and the two men jogged inside.

On the other side of the city, on top of the wall, a few yards away from John and Vince, Cakk was sweating with fear and frustration. He was still fumbling with the cannon's wires.

"How's it coming, bro?" Wilson asked. He could see more aliens converging on Beri and Hilton's location. The plan was working, driving half of the aliens away from the castle. The other half was scampering into the castle to protect their leader. Unfortunately, if the cannon were not fixed in time, Beri and Hilton would not survive the onslaught.

A crackle sounded through Wilson's communicator.

"A little help here!" Hilton said. "What's going on with the cannon?"

"I'm working on it!" Cakk shouted.

Hilton ran into a nearby house looking for a safe place to talk with Cakk. He quickly scaled a flight of stairs into an upper room and began to take a few shots through a window at oncoming aliens. Hilton put his communicator to his ear.

Cakk, still struggling in the tiny space of the cannon bay, tried to explain the electrical mess in front of him. "Four wires, all different colors, severed in the middle."

"How are they situated at the top and bottom?" asked Hilton.

Wilson turned away from the sights and grabbed the communicator from Cakk. "Four on the top, all in a row, but two on each side."

"Okay," Hilton said, trying to think. Just then he saw Beri half sprinting, half limping, across one of the side streets, firing into the pack of aliens, drawing a quarter of them toward her. She must have overheard Hilton's conversation with Cakk through the communicator and decided he needed a little more time. The only problem now was Hilton would have to defend himself against a stampede of aliens alone if this cannon didn't work soon.

The aliens chattered amongst themselves and their voices echoed off of the throne room's marble floor and into Maco's ear holes. He retorted and a few of the aliens silenced. Altaira looked at the aliens, waiting for their next move.

"As you wish," Maco responded to Altaira's command. The throne room doors opened and all the aliens, save for Maco left the room.

Altaira was cautious of his response. Maco turned to her and said, "You will be a good leader." He started to leave the room, and then he paused.

"You think so, Maco?"

"Yes," he assured her. He turned to leave the room again, but he paused again. "Just one question, Queen Altaira."

"Yes?"

"Since our forces are divided, how many should we apply to the wall?"

Altaira had no idea how many aliens there were, so this question seemed out of place. Maco knew she would not know the size of his army and his question was an affirmation of that fact.

"How many do we have?" Altaira asked, playing Maco's strange game.

"Let's see," he said. He turned to chatter with the aliens that were just beyond the throne room doors. Then Maco turned and began to walk toward Altaira. Alien after alien entered the room behind Maco, walking slowly toward the throne. The aliens filled almost every space in the room except for the throne, covering the entire floor.

Altaira, feeling uneasy at the sheer number of aliens around her, estimated that there were at least a thousand beings in this room.

"Do you think that is enough?" Maco asked sinisterly.

John raced into the underground palace dungeons. Vince followed as closely as he could. There were no aliens in these parts of the castle because very few people knew about these corridors. They were used years ago by ancient dynasties to hold war criminals. Admiral Raynger had only learned of these cells because Lyonne natives like John had betrayed their own. John knew who was down here – some of the most powerful people on Planet York III.

As John turned a last corner, he stopped in awe. The long corridor, dimly lit by blue lights, was filled with people in cells. There were more people down here than John had even suspected. He turned to Vince and recited four numbers.

"Four-nine-six-one."

"Let all of them out?" Vince questioned.

"All of them," John reassured him. "But we must find Atlanta or Francesca Marquette first.

"Who are they?"

"The rightful queens of Planet York III."

Fifteen floors above in the palace, Altaira sat uneasily on the throne. She knew something was coming, but still she was unprepared for it. Aliens began charging the throne. There were so many that she could barely see Maco leaving the room. She could, however, hear his last words.

"Kill her!"

Altaira held out her hands and blasted a pack of aliens off the side of the throne. She began to leap into the air, but she was quickly dragged down to the floor by six aliens pulling on her purple cape. A few staffs fell across the back of her head, making her vision blur for a moment. The number of aliens was overwhelming her and they were coming from all directions. Altaira broke away and swooped to the vaulted ceiling of the throne room, carrying four aliens with her. She crashed into the wall, knocking the aliens from her back. The impact sent her falling back to the floor. More aliens continued to flood the room, piling on top of Altaira. One of the aliens reached for one of the bracelets and ripped it off. Instantly Altaira felt weaker.

She forced herself into a standing position, throwing five aliens off her, and searched the chaos for the golden bracelet. As she was looking, another alien ripped the other bracelet off her wrist. Altaira collapsed and her glow faded even more. A few more blows to the head and back all but crumpled her to the marble floor. She started to close her eyes from fatigue as she felt her purple cape being ripped from her back. Altaira's strength was fading fast. She needed help. She couldn't do this alone.

Deep in the pits of the castle, John shouted at the top of his lungs over the crazed prisoners. They had been down here for a long time and they could sense that these two intruders were not here to kill them. They shouted toward John and Vince to let them be free.

"Atlanta Marquette! Francesca Marquette!" John and Vince shouted.

They repeated their plea over and over again. Feeling frustrated, John and Vince reached the end of the corridor. They found two opposing cells, each with one woman inside.

"Of course they're here," John said.

He and Vince opened the cells. The two women who emerged were almost identical – except one had red hair and the other brown. They were definitely twin sisters. John, having not seen either woman for ages, wasn't sure which woman was Atlanta or Francesca, so he took a guess.

"My queen," he said toward Atlanta with a slight bow.

"Enough!" Francesca responded. "What is going on? Who is attacking us?"

John turned toward the correct queen and answered. "We have been attacked by Maco and his legion."

Instantly knowing what to do, Francesca pointed to one of the cells at the opposite end of the corridor. She and her sister walked briskly toward the cell followed by John and Vince. When Francesca approached the panel, she entered a code unfamiliar to John and all of the cell doors slid open. There was a simultaneous cheer from the captives as they realized their freedom was restored.

"Long live Queen Marquette!" they cried in unison.

John quietly asked Atlanta, "That code?"

"Its an override that only Francesca and I know."

Then a huge man, standing about seven feet and ten inches tall, weighing easily three hundred pounds of pure muscle, emerged from the back of the cell. His presence seemed sinister, until he kneeled in front of Francesca.

"General Xenrock," Francesca said with a smile. "So good to see you again."

"And you as well, my queen."

"We have been attacked by Maco," she explained. "He has come for my throne. Take those who are strong enough to fight and restore a perimeter around the city. Atlanta," she said turning to her sister. "I'll take the other half and head toward the throne. You stay with the general. We don't have much time."

As the general pointed out people whom he deemed fit to follow, Vince leaned toward John and said, "But they have no weapons."

Atlanta retorted, "They don't need weapons."

Vince wasn't sure what she meant by her comment, but clearly she and the others didn't fear death.

John leaned toward Francesca and humbly asked, "What about us?" Francesca turned to notice the questioning eyes of John and Vince, looking like pets that had strayed too far from their masters.

"You've done enough, John. Fighting is not for scientists," she said with a condescending tone. She wiped a spot of blood from his brow and turned to follow the rest of the prisoners out of the chambers.

As the last of the prisoners went storming out, Vince and John turned to look at each other. Before John could say anything, Vince said, "I think she likes you."

"I need some help here!" Wilson shouted through the communicator. "That last combination didn't work."

"Blasted thing!" Cakk shouted back.

"I wish it would blast something," Hilton said trying to think. The aliens were beginning to converge on his location. It was only a matter of time before they would storm into the house and find him alone. He dared not think what they would do to him if they captured him.

"Try reversing the combination," Hilton shouted back.

Wilson quickly untied the wires and reversed the pairings. Cakk glanced through the cannon's sights only to see the aliens getting closer to Hilton's location. He couldn't see Beri anywhere. He could only hope she was safe.

"We could really use back up right now," Hilton muttered to himself.

He could see a few weak blasts from Beri's weapon between the houses on the far side of the street. She seemed to be doing okay, but the power in her weapon would only last for a few more minutes. There was no sign that John, Vince, or Altaira were successful in their part of the plan.

Then a group of about fifty people came charging out from a lower level of the castle. They swarmed around the aliens and the aliens had to turn around to face these new attackers. Hilton wasn't sure who these people were, but at this point any distraction to draw the aliens away from him was welcome. These new attackers were stronger, faster, and seemed impervious to pain. Some of them moved so fast between alien attackers that he couldn't believe how they could dodge, punch, and steal a weapon in one full move. No amount of military training could teach that. These new attackers didn't seem human.

Hilton shook off his amazement and decided to tell Beri what was happening. "Captain Onex! Are you seeing this?"

There was no response.

"Beri!" Hilton shouted again into the communicator.

"Yes, Hilton, I see them." she responded. "The cavalry is here!"

"They are moving fast!"

"I gave them your location, so just stay put. We don't want any friendly fire."

Hilton wasn't sure what Beri meant, but he soon noticed they were talking about two different things.

Blast after blast began raining down from the sky. The deafening sounds of engines roared around Hilton. He stuck his head out of the broken window in the rundown house to see seven Light Rippers swooping down out of the red mid-morning sky. Three bigger freighters, called Dusk Destroyers, followed those smaller aircraft. The cavalry was indeed here. Hilton ducked back into the house, collapsed onto the floor in a sitting position and breathed a heavy sigh of relief. Home was not far away anymore.

Altaira struggled to fight off the increasing number of attacking aliens. Each time she pushed off two or three, more came in to continue the fight. Her energy was fading and surprisingly, so was her size. She was getting closer to the ground, both in posture and height.

Finally she collapsed completely on to the cold, hard floor. Her eyes were all but closed. There was, however, a small enough crease to let one single tear fall to the marble floor. Altaira wasn't crying in pain, in fact she felt very little pain. She was sad, regretful that she may have brought this chaos into a world she had only begun to live in and barely understood. There was something wrong about all this, yet Altaira couldn't stop it.

Or could she?

Somewhere inside her she felt a calming peace. Inside her a void began to form, growing larger as she continued to shrink. Eventually her size got so small that the aliens stopped beating her, and a few fell to the floor underneath her. She was now hovering slightly over the floor, rising little by little off the marble floor. Altaira couldn't see anything but a bright golden light that was fading into a white, solemn blue. The sounds around her began to fade, until she heard nothing anymore.

All of the aliens stared at this sight with disbelief. The ones standing did not move, and the ones lying on the floor sat up to get a better view of this spectacle. Without warning, this female being they had been fighting was now transformed into a small sphere, not much bigger than a marble, floating three feet above the marble floor. There was a dim light glowing from within this sphere that merged from gold to white to blue and back to gold.

Suddenly, without warning, Francesca and her group of fighters stormed into the throne room. They were ready to fight, but the aliens didn't seem interested. They continued to stare at this tiny glowing sphere as if mesmerized by it. One of the fighters with Francesca started to attack, but she stopped him.

"I think we should leave," Francesca said in a calming voice, turning to leave the throne room.

Just before she could relay the message to the rest of her group, the tiny sphere expanded, doubling in its size, and instantly retracted into its original size.

"Run!" Francesca screamed.

A mass panic ensued. The humans with Francesca turned and bolted back into the lower levels of the palace. The aliens who seemed to understand her command began to scramble for the door. Looking for the safest place, Francesca wrapped her arms around a tall, stone pillar just outside the throne room entrance. The tiny sphere repeated its expansion and contraction again, only this time it disappeared. Then the explosion happened.

The explosion was not of fire and heat, but rather of wind, light, and energy. Francesca turned her eyes away and gripped the pillar in fear. A few aliens and humans were sent flying into the air, smashing through windows and into walls. The ceiling of the castle cracked in half and rock began to shoot into the sky. The entire palace shook, causing pillars to break and collapse. Screams could be heard from those who were hurt or killed by the explosion. Outside the palace a few Light Rippers crash-landed into the city streets.

The sphere created a gravitational vortex and began to pull everything toward it. The dimly lit vortex spun in a counterclockwise direction and created a small tornado of wind. The energy it had projected was now being reclaimed. Rock and dust were the first things to be sucked into the vortex. Soon after went the closest aliens, screaming as they disappeared into the black hole. Francesca grabbed the pillar even harder as she felt her legs lift up off of the floor and begin to pull her toward the vortex. She saw a few of her best fighters struggle against the gravitational force, only to be taken into the darkness amidst screams and pleas for mercy.

As her grip loosened, the queen closed her eyes, hoping that her fate would not be such. The pillar she clung to was starting to break away from the ceiling. Then it broke completely, half of it soaring into the black vortex that was getting stronger. The piece that Francesca held onto smashed into the floor and was dragged toward the vortex. She could hear people screaming her name, begging for help. "Queen Marquette!"

Then as if the vortex heard their plea, it was gone instantly, imploding into itself. Dust and rock, aliens and people, anything that was suspended in air moving toward the vortex dropped painfully to the floor. The queen, her arms and hands hurting from gripping the pillar so hard, relaxed and turned over onto her back. She could see high above the sparse clouds a Sci-Fi Force Ray Patroller hovering outside of Planet York III's atmosphere. The massive ship brought a temporary sense of relief to the queen, but that feeling would change soon enough.

The Final Chapter

"Vara!" John shouted as he burst through the tattered door into the dilapidated house. "We won!"

There was no response. Only the sound of weeping could be heard. Lilac came from the back of the house, her wounded shoulder limp at her side. She walked slowly toward John, not saying anything. Then she stopped directly in front of him. She handed him an old notebook covered with dust and smelling of smoke.

"We found this," Lilac said. "We think he would have wanted you to have it."

John grasped the binder. Lilac exited the room slowly without another word. John knew what had happened. Dr. Nolan had died. Vara, who was like his only child, was distraught. John decided to give her some space. He turned and exited the house, sat down outside on the dusty road, and began to look at the pages in the professor's notebook. A few tears fell from his eyes and dampened the pages.

Lieutenant Commander McGraw of Sci-Fi Force stared at Queen Marquette with a very serious look on his face, which was normal for those who knew him well.

"I regret to inform you, Lieutenant, we will not be needing any more support from the Sci-Fi Force organization," Francesca said sternly.

The queen stood at the bottom of the grand staircase to the now half-destroyed palace. Immediately behind her was her sister, Atlanta, followed by a group of thirty humans who were a mixture of Lyonne's palace guards and top commanders.

"But what of this Maco?" the lieutenant asked. "If he should return, how will you defend yourselves?"

"We managed before, and I'm sure we can in the future. It was Admiral Raynger who tipped the tide against us all and then refused to give the people of Planet York III a chance to rule themselves."

"I'm sorry you see it that way," McGraw cautioned. "Admiral Raynger has been dead for some time. He did not authorize stationing troops on your planet." The queen did not respond. She was waiting for more answers.

"Admiral Raynger was killed when a captain aboard his ship created a mutiny. All of the loyal Sci-Fi Force agents aboard the Ray Patroller were gassed with a deadly disease and left to die," McGraw explained, showing no emotion.

Even though the story sounded slightly believable, Francesca paused. She vaguely remembered her father, King Mirage Marquette, talking fondly of Admiral Raynger and how he had helped him keep Maco's alien army at bay.

Before Francesca could ask another question, Atlanta blurted out, "What was the captain's name?"

"Captain Nammill," the lieutenant responded.

"Well, there you are," Hilton said, smiling as Lilac approached.

Hilton was sitting on a crate next to the loading plank of one of the Dusk Destroyers. The midday sun was beginning to get hot and Hilton's brow began to sweat. He didn't mind though. A few moments of quiet were well received.

As Lilac got closer to him, one of the Sci-Fi Force medics rushed over to her, grabbed her good arm, and began to lead her into the huge freighter.

"Senior Agent Wenn. We'd better take a good look at that shoulder," he said.

"Senior Agent?" she asked surprisingly.

"Congratulations," Hilton said with a smile. "From one newly promoted agent to another."

As Lilac disappeared into the large spaceship, Hilton turned to look at Beri, who was standing just out of earshot, talking to Chief Captain Sheep.

"Sounds like you have a lot to report, Captain."

"Yes, sir," she responded. "We lost two agents, but I think there might be other things that were going on here."

"Yes?"

"There might be some new species on this planet, ones that are not logged in the Sci-Fi Force databases," she cautioned. She wished that Penn were still alive. He could better explain the scientific stuff.

"Well," Chief Captain Sheep said, selecting his words carefully, "As long as they stay here on this planet."

Beri was surprised at his response. Sci-Fi Force was always concerned when new species were discovered. It was a defensive posture they had taken for thousands of years just in case something ever evolved that they couldn't contain.

"We have been given orders by the queen to eradicate this planet from our jurisdiction. This was the only planet in the QX sector that paid for our support," Chief Captain Sheep revealed to Beri.

"So we will have to abandon the entire sector?"

Captain Sheep's silence was affirmative. As Beri's superior turned to leave her, she could only think about Altaira. Questions flowed through her head. What was Altaira? Did the professor really create her by himself, and if he did, could someone else repeat the process?

"She was a star!" John exclaimed, rushing back into the house.

He ran into the room where the dead professor lay and where Vara's brothers were comforting her. Cakk wasn't sure what the commotion was about, but he didn't want his sister rattled. He turned to block John, but he pushed past him. Vara looked up from the embrace of her older brother.

"Altaira was a star," John repeated. "The professor created a living, breathing star, mixed with his DNA. He created life that could survive in deep space." Cakk scratched his head in confusion. Vara and Wilson were interested in John's discovery.

John held out one of Altaira's golden bracelets. The jewelry was now dirty and scarred. "These bracelets helped her maintain her internal gravitational pull," John explained.

Vara, catching up slowly, wiped tears from her cheeks. Wilson now looked just as confused as Cakk.

"When she lost these, she could no longer maintain the strength to control her gravitational vortex."

John, noticing that they were not understanding, continued, "So when she exploded, that created an inverted gravitational pull."

"Pulling everything toward her," Vara said, wiping a few tears from her face, but still not sure of the relevance of the conversation.

Cakk and Wilson were confused as to why John's demeanor was so jovial. After all, they were in a room with a dead body. John sighed, frustrated that they didn't see where he was headed.

"Matter can never be created or destroyed. It just changes into other things."

"But where does a star go when it dies?" Vara asked, trying to understand John's point.

"To its source," John said, turning to leave.

"Where are you going?" Vara asked.

"To find Altaira," John said, clutching Dr. Nolan's notebook.

Vara let go of her brother's grasp. "I'm coming with you."

Cakk and Wilson watched as the two quickly walked out of the abandoned house. They both looked at each other.

"Wait for us!" they said running after their sister.

Epilogue

The bright morning sun broke through the castle bedroom in which the Queen of Lyonne slept. This room, however, was not the queen's actual bedroom. That room was still under repair and had been for the last few months. Francesca rolled over, turning away from the window that let in the crease of light. The queen lay there trying to go back to sleep. She couldn't help but hear clamoring throughout the palace. It sounded as if the chefs were early at work preparing her breakfast, but they were definitely noisier than normal. Suddenly one of her palace guards crashed into her room.

"Sorry, your highness," the female guard said. "We have some unusual visitors here. They want to speak to you."

There had been months of peace in Lyonne and its surrounding cities since the war with Maco's aliens had ended. The queen was not in the mood for silly games and nonsense. This alarm was definitely serious, however. Francesca leapt out of her bed and quickly got dressed. She grabbed her father's shock spear on the way out of the bedroom, just in case.

As she neared the front entrance of the palace, she was blinded by a light that radiated into the main corridor. Francesca shielded her eyes as she stepped out onto the terrace at the top of the steps. She blinked a few times to regain her sight.

Still squinting, she glanced to her right, where she saw her sister Atlanta, standing in an attack position, holding her own shock spear, but not moving. To her left were four palace guards, their faces showing nothing but fear. In front of here were five creatures that she had only seen the likeness of once before. There were four females, each standing beside a large male in the center. They all glowed just like Altaira.

The closest female to the right of the large male spoke, "We are the Shooting Stars and we have already conquered every other planet and moon in this system. Your planet is the last on our list."

Queen Marquette didn't say a word.

The large, glowing male in the center showed a confident, sinister smile. He winked at her.

CPSIA information can be obtained
at www.ICGtesting.com
Printed in the USA
LVHW081345181122
733436LV00016B/977